Emily stared spellbound at the man beside her.

Sonny Maxwell. *The* Sonny Maxwell. And he'd saved her from drowning.

It didn't seem possible, but he was even more beautiful in person. It wasn't his looks that mesmerized her, though. It was the soft glow of light she could sense shimmering around him.

White, with a hint of gray... The color confused her. A person like Sonny Maxwell couldn't have such an aura.

His hand was still grasping hers. She looked down. Beneath his fingertips, where their skin touched, was a warm lavender glow.

Lavender. The color of humanity.

Dazed, confused, she looked up from their joined hands. "You...you're white...." she said, forcing the words through frozen lips. A gust of wind cut through her, and she shivered violently.

His eyes narrowed with concern. "You're blue. And getting bluer."

"You c-can s-see auras, t-too?"

"Auras?" A shiver shook his shoulders. He muttered something about signs of delirium, then shoved himself to his feet, extending a hand to her. "Come on. We've got to get moving."

Dear Reader,

Happy holidays! Though it may be cold outside, it's always warmed by the festivities of this special season. Everyone at Silhouette Books wishes you joy and cheer at this wonderful time of the year.

In December, we have some heartwarming books to take the chill off the weather. The final title in our DIAMOND JUBILEE celebration is *Only the Nanny Knows for Sure* by Phyllis Halldorson. Don't miss this tender love story about a nanny who has a secret . . . and a handsome hero who doesn't stand a ghost of a chance at remaining a bachelor!

The DIAMOND JUBILEE—Silhouette Romance's tenth anniversary celebration—is our way of saying thanks to you, our readers. To symbolize the timelessness of love, as well as the modern gift of the tenth anniversary, we've presented readers with a DIAMOND JUBILEE Silhouette Romance each month in 1990, penned by one of your favorite Silhouette Romance authors. It's been a wonderful year of love and romance here at Silhouette Books, and we hope that you've enjoyed our DIAMOND JUBILEE celebration. Saying thanks has never been so much fun!

And that's not all! There are six books a month from Silhouette Romance—stories by wonderful writers who time and time again bring home the magic of love. And we've got a lot of exciting events planned for 1991. In January, look for Marie Ferrarella's *The Undoing of Justin Starbuck*—the first book in the WRITTEN IN THE STARS series. Each month in 1991, we're proud to present readers with a book that focuses on the hero—and his Zodiac sign. Be sure to watch for that mysterious Capricorn man . . . and then meet Mr. Aquarius in *Man from the North Country* by Laurie Paige in February.

1991 is sure to be extra special. With works by authors such as Diana Palmer (don't miss her upcoming Long, Tall Texan!), Annette Broadrick, Nora Roberts and so many other talented writers, how could it not be? It's always celebration time at Silhouette Romance— the celebration of love.

I hope you'll enjoy this book and all of the stories to come. Come home to romance—Silhouette Romance—for always!

Sincerely,

Tara Gavin
Senior Editor

THERESA WEIR

Pictures of Emily

Silhouette Romance
Published by Silhouette Books New York
America's Publisher of Contemporary Romance

To those people
who help keep me on the right track,
especially Kim, Linda, Sue and Janice—
thanks.

SILHOUETTE BOOKS
300 E. 42nd St., New York, N.Y. 10017

ISBN: 0-373-08761-6

First Silhouette Books printing December 1990
Second Silhouette Books printing January 1991

Printed in the U.S.A.

Books by Theresa Weir

Silhouette Romance

The Forever Man #576
Loving Jenny #650
Pictures of Emily #761

Silhouette Intimate Moments

Iguana Bay #339

THERESA WEIR

lives on an apple, cattle and sheep farm in Illinois, not far from the Mississippi River. She was a 1988 Romantic Writers of America Golden Medallion finalist for her first book, *The Forever Man*, a Silhouette Romance. She is also the winner of the 1988 *Romantic Times* New Romantic Adventure Writer Award.

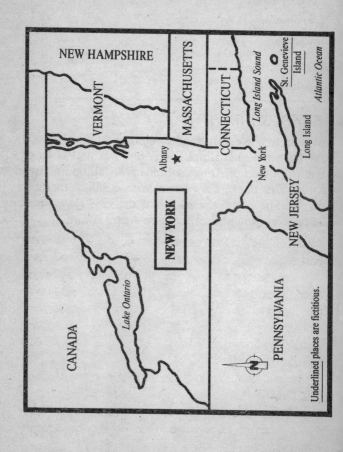

CANADA

Lake Ontario

NEW YORK

Albany ★

VERMONT

NEW HAMPSHIRE

MASSACHUSETTS

CONNECTICUT

Long Island Sound

St. Genevieve Island

Atlantic Ocean

Long Island

New York

NEW JERSEY

PENNSYLVANIA

N

Underlined places are fictitious.

Chapter One

A damp east coast wind bit across Doreen Mc-Donald's lined cheeks, creeping down the upturned collar of her jacket, penetrating all the way to her bones. She was pushing sixty—too old for these location shoots. Lord, how she wished the magazine hadn't sent them to this godforsaken little island to do the layout. Her sinuses ached and the joints in her fingers were stiff. She should have packed a winter coat, but who would have thought it could be so cold the end of April?

She muttered, cursing the wind that blew off the chill North Atlantic waters. She checked her light meter, readjusted the aperture setting, then made sure the tripod-steadied camera was still focused on Sonny Maxwell.

It was.

He was leaning negligently against one of the algae-covered boulders that littered the rocky point, hands jammed deep into the pockets of his leather flight jacket, facing the setting sun. If the earth were flat, they may have been able to see Long Island—Doreen's home. Civilization. It lay approximately sixty miles west, over the curve of the water. But she could be almost certain Sonny wasn't yearning for home. He hadn't vocalized any opinion, but she sensed that he liked it here. And now he was watching the sun make a spectacle of itself, setting so gloriously out there in the icy North Atlantic. The wind tugged at his shaggy, sun-streaked mane, whipping the thick blunt ends against his white shirt collar. Below him, waves pounded smooth black rocks, spraying salt water on his faded jeans.

"Perfect," Doreen said, squinting through the viewfinder. "I can just catch the lighthouse in the corner of the frame."

Of course, any female over age twelve would tell you it wasn't the lighthouse that mattered. It was Sonny Maxwell. And photographing Sonny Maxwell was pure pleasure, weather and location aside.

Doreen was one of the only photographers who preferred to work without a crew. Maybe that's why she and Sonny got along so well. He was one of the only big names who didn't travel with an entourage. Because of their compatibility, Doreen took all his photos. And since he refused to have an agent or manager, she was also his unofficial advisor.

"Come on, Sonny!" She had to shout in order to be heard over the sound of the surf. "Let's see that heartbreakingly aloof look you're so famous for. The one that makes all those female knees turn to jelly and their little hearts go pitter-patter."

Sonny's head came around and he coolly eyed the camera.

Most models, even the biggest names, had a self-consciousness that could be picked up on film. The trick was to catch them in that fragment of a second when they forgot themselves, when something else flickered across their minds. Sonny was the only person Doreen had ever worked with who wasn't intimidated by the camera lens. Not because he was so totally confident about his looks, but because he just didn't give a damn.

Right now a mocking smile played about his sensuous mouth. "You know, Doreen, the shot would be better without the lighthouse in the background."

His voice carried easily above the sound of crashing waves.

In all the years she'd known him, Doreen couldn't remember hearing him raise his voice. He didn't need to. It had a deep, resonant timbre that just kind of reverberated in your chest, around your heart. Made you melt a little inside.

"I'm the photographer," she reminded him. "You're the model, remember?"

"The lighthouse is too obvious. Move your frame to the left, catch the crag there."

She knew he was goading her. One thing she couldn't stand was being told how to set up a shot. "You should have gotten a haircut before coming to this godforsaken place," she said. "I like your hair long, but it won't appeal to everybody."

Who was she kidding? She was old enough to be his mother—almost old enough to be his grandmother, if the truth was told—and everything about him appealed to her. Several years ago, when they'd first met and Doreen had had one too many cocktails at a photo showing, she'd invited him up to her apartment. He'd smoothly declined, saying he didn't want to ruin a good working relationship. And strangely enough, they'd been friends ever since. If Sonny Maxwell called anybody his friend.

"And shave," she said. "Tomorrow, shave."

"Go to hell, Doreen."

The shutter clicked. "I love you, too, sweetheart. The rugged look is great, but when we get home, I want to have some wholesome shots."

"I don't do wholesome shots."

How true. Sonny was what she thought of as a casualty of the industry. A fatherless child raised by a selfish, alcoholic mother. It made her heart ache, yet she knew he despised pity.

He smiled, and the reflection from the setting sun caught his eyes, making his face suddenly seem alive, eager, full of life. And Doreen was struck by the irony of it.

The shutter clicked again. And again.

"How about sitting on top of that rock. Look out at the ocean and brood, or I guess I should say act natural."

With the sole of one booted foot, Sonny pushed himself away from the boulder to stand facing her, legs splayed. And now the sun no longer reflected from his eyes. They were the same calm gray they had always been. "What do you say we wrap it up? Go get a drink?"

Sonny noticed little things. He was considerate. And now Doreen wondered if he'd noticed her teeth chattering a while ago, if that's why he was suggesting they wrap up.

She focused and pressed the shutter release a few more times. "Yeah, maybe we should. The light's getting weird."

With one hand she pushed at her irritatingly straight bangs—the only part of her coarse salt-and-pepper hair that was over an inch long. "Lord, I'll be glad to feel concrete under my feet again." She unscrewed the lens from the camera and put it in the soft case, then removed the camera from the tripod. "Why the hell couldn't the magazine have sent us to Nantucket, or Martha's Vineyard, or some halfway civilized place with some sort of nightlife?"

Sonny laughed and Doreen shivered.

"Stop that," she said.

"Stop what?"

"You know I hate it when you laugh like that." His laugh contained so much bitterness and mockery. Almost as if he mocked life itself. And coming from such a face. Angels shouldn't be bitter.

It was no accident that they were here in this remote fishing village. The advertising editor of the hip, music-oriented magazine had chosen the island because it was wild and forbidding. Isolated. Like Sonny, she'd said.

They were working on an advertising campaign for a line of expensive leather jackets. Leather jackets and Sonny were a powerful combination. Together they created an incredibly sexy image. And that's what it was all about.

Sonny was a commodity. People used him, played his emotions, his face, his body, for all they were worth, wringing everything out of him until there was nothing left.

Yet he kept playing the game.

Doreen had once asked him why, and he'd gotten the strangest look on his face, then laughed his mocking laugh, saying that modeling clothes was what he did best.

He'd made a couple of movies, but the critics had torn him to ribbons. Directors said he was difficult to work with. They complained that he was too stiff, too controlled. He didn't show enough emotion.

In a way she supposed it was true, what Sonny said about modeling being what he did best, because it was the frozen stills that captured his essence.

Sonny picked up the tripod. With sure, dexterous fingers, he loosened the legs and telescoped them away.

Something on the horizon caught his attention, the setting sun, perhaps. He stood there a moment, looking out past the breakers.

Watching him, Doreen thought again how strange it was for a model to have achieved such fame. He didn't really fit the standard macho hunk image. He wasn't big and muscular. But then, big, muscular men didn't wear clothes well. Sonny wore clothes well. Very well. His body was lean and taut and well-honed. Perfect. And his hands. His hands made her think of a pianist's, they were that long, that sensitive-looking. She wondered how many millions of women had dreamed of those hands. . . .

But it wasn't just his looks that had gotten him voted one of the world's ten sexiest men for the last three years. Ironically enough, it was the emotions he thought he so carefully disguised that made his photos what they were. Because the camera was fast. It could see and record things undetectable to the human eye. And because of that, the camera was able to penetrate his skin, to probe the furthest reaches of his soul so it was exposed for all to see. The cynicism, the mockery, the calm acceptance. The pain. It was all there.

But perhaps the most compelling thing about him was the pure sensuality that was so frustratingly combined with the untouchableness.

And those eyes. Those eyes were really something special. They were heavy-lidded, which made him look a little sleepy—or made him look as if he'd just been making love to some lucky woman.

But sometimes Doreen caught herself reading something in them she didn't want to see. Bleakness. Sonny was someone who had seen the world as a stark place, a cruel place, and had accepted it as such. And who could really blame him?

He wasn't materialistic. He'd driven the same jeep for years. He owned a cabin and a few acres of land somewhere in New York State. He didn't allow anyone to go there. Doreen didn't even know where it was. But when he wasn't working, she imagined him living a back to basics, Walden Pond sort of existence.

Once when she'd asked him what he did with all the money he made, he'd shrugged and smiled, then said he blew it. Later, by accident, she'd found out that he'd used it to help add a children's wing to a hospital. And though she didn't know for certain, she suspected that he'd done more of the same.

Deep. You're deep, my Sonny boy.

Standing next to him, almost brushing his shoulder, Doreen could feel Sonny's isolation, like a wall. A wall constructed by chubby child hands that had eventually grown into sensitive adult hands. A wall painstakingly raised brick by brick, year by year, to finally stand a relic to a cold, loveless childhood.

With a graceful, fluid movement, Sonny bent and picked up the camera case. Then, side by side, they struck out toward the village.

Doreen liked to walk and the village was just the right distance away, no more than a quarter of a mile if they stayed on the winding path that cut through sand dunes topped by tufts of rustling grass. As they walked, Doreen's circulation began to improve, the increase in blood flow bringing warmth to her toes and fingers.

When they reached the narrow cobblestone street that led to the quaint, very New England town square, Sonny paused beneath a creaking pub sign. Hair blowing across his forehead, he looked up at the woodcut of a frothy stein of beer. "Feel like a drink?"

Cold beer was the last thing Doreen wanted and even though she knew the pub had Irish coffee, she declined. What she needed was a good hot soak in the tub. And it wasn't as if Sonny hated to drink alone. Sometimes she suspected that he preferred it.

He handed the tripod and camera case to her. "Go take a hot bath. I'll meet you later for dinner."

"Stop treating me like an old woman," she said, the fear of getting old welling within her.

"You're not old."

"I'll be sixty in three years," she challenged.

"Like I said, you're not old."

It was useless to argue about such a ridiculous thing. Instead, she nodded in order to placate him. Whatever he said, sixty *was* old. Nothing could change that.

She turned toward the inn, worrying that her age was beginning to slow her down. She was getting tired of struggling to remain near the top. There were so many bright, innovative kids out there, just waiting. Full of energy. The kind of energy she used to have. Maybe she should just step aside, let them have their chance. But photography wasn't something she could just walk away from. It was as vital to her as oxygen.

And if she quit, what would happen to Sonny? Who would protect him from the vultures?

Sonny watched Doreen move away through the dampness. He realized with a sudden jolt that her hair was more gray than black. When had that happened? Why hadn't he noticed before? It suddenly seemed that she'd aged ten years in the last one. And she seemed to have shrunk a little.

Was she taking care of herself? Eating right? It wasn't like him to get personal, not even with Doreen, but he was worried about her. He'd make sure she got a physical when they returned to the mainland. That decision made, he felt a little better.

Sonny was ready to duck into the pub when he saw the kite. It was so high he couldn't make out its shape, couldn't tell what it was supposed to be. Yesterday's kite had been some sort of fairy creature. He'd been on the island long enough to know that Emily Christian, the village kite maker, put out a kite with the sunrise and brought it in with the sunset. Through the day, it flew unattended, tied to a piling at the dock's end.

Sonny didn't go into the pub.

Instead, hands jammed into the front pockets of his jeans, he headed toward the wharf, where the kite string led.

The wharf extended a good eighth of a mile into the ocean and was wide enough for a car to drive down.

It smelled of fish and salt water and wood that had been soaked in creosote. There were little shops scattered here and there, but they were all closed since the summer tourist season hadn't yet started.

But it wasn't the shops that drew Sonny.

He stopped in front of a closed bait shop and looked toward the end of the wharf, the length of a football field away.

She was there.

Flying her kite above the ocean. Dark sky above, dark water below. Suspended between two powerful elements...or maybe a part of them. Watching, Sonny felt something he hadn't felt in years: curiosity.

Most of the people who knew him would probably be surprised to discover that Sonny Maxwell viewed the world through the eyes of an artist. He liked pictures that told stories, created a single mood. The woman with the kite did both.

Sonny never analyzed his feelings by putting them into words. If he had, he would have said that the picture before him was pure old-fashioned enchantment.

The kite. The ocean. The darkening sky with just a streak of red. The blustery wind. The woman. Or woman-child with her billowing hair and long heavy skirt.

Like the village she lived in, she seemed untouched by time and modern ways.

Her hair was thick and blond and wavy, and would have reached past her waist if it hadn't been pulled by the wind, rippling it behind her like a delicate banner.

Mermaid's hair.

Even from this distance, he could tell that her clothes looked as if they could have been from another period. They were coarse, dark, heavy, most likely made of wool, most likely homespun. On her feet she wore leather boots that stopped at her ankles.

Yesterday he'd asked the innkeeper about her, and the man had instantly become suspicious. When he finally told Sonny who she was and what she did, his answer had come reluctantly.

Sonny was well aware of the villagers' reactions to his and Doreen's presence in their little isolated community. They were anxious for them to leave. They were afraid. Even though they made money off the summer tourists, they didn't associate with them, didn't want the outsiders' morals rubbing off on their children.

So Sonny hung back.

Which wasn't hard for him to do. He'd spent his life hanging back, quietly watching. On the outside, looking in. And that was the way he preferred it.

Now, watching the woman, he could fully understand the innkeeper's protectiveness.

Doreen loved to photograph people. All sorts of people. Unusual people. But Sonny hoped Doreen wouldn't see this woman.

Sonny had read somewhere that early American Indians wouldn't allow photographers to take pictures of them because they believed their soul became trapped within the printed image. Superstitious nonsense to some, but Sonny knew it was true.

Doreen would do more than take pictures of Emily, she would send them—little pieces of Emily Christian's soul—to New York where they would lay on the desks of magazine publishers. Where they would be touched. Examined in a most clinical manner.

And he knew once they saw Emily Christian, they would want her. And if they got her...

An unfamiliar emotion twisted deep inside him. Pain, or maybe fear. Whatever it was, it made no sense so he pushed it aside and absorbed the scene before him.

Today's kite was just as colorful as yesterday's. But where yesterday's had been red, this one was a shimmering emerald green. As the mermaid reeled it in, Sonny recognized it as a dragon with wings that had to span at least six feet. A bumpy tail fluttered beneath fierce talons.

How could such a thing possibly fly? It looked too bulky. And what was she using for string? High-test fishing line?

As the giant creature came lower, a recalcitrant wind caught it, whipped it, pulled it. The woman fought to keep the kite under control, fought to keep the beautiful masterpiece from diving into the ocean.

Sonny didn't consciously think about helping, but suddenly his boots were pounding across the wooden wharf. As the distance between them closed, the kite dipped once more, then plunged below his line of vision, into the choppy, icy waters.

The woman herself lunged, grabbed at air, then toppled forward to disappear over the side of the dock.

Sonny heard a scream, then nothing but the roar of the ocean.

He shed his coat as he raced toward the end of the wharf. As he moved, his mind sped faster.

Could she swim? Her clothes were heavy, would hold water, pull her down. The water was cold, frigid. Fifty degrees, tops.

He reached the end of the wharf and jerked off his boots, taking in everything at once.

The woman was fighting, struggling to keep her head above water, but the weight of her saturated clothes was too much for her. Her long hair had also turned into an enemy, ensnaring her arms.

Sonny dove. The shock of the icy water stole the breath from his lungs. He surfaced, gasping, his fingers groping. He managed to latch onto a handful of wet clothing. He dragged her through the water toward him, trying to turn her face up as he pulled.

Sonny felt her convulse. She wheezed. Choked. Then in a floundering panic, she wrapped her arms around him, shoving his head under water.

Suddenly the attempted rescue turned into a battle for both their lives. He fought her, finally tearing her clamped hands from his arms. He surfaced, filling his lungs with air. Treading water, he managed to force her around so she was unable to cling to him.

He cast a quick glance toward the pier. It was a good six feet from the surface of the water to the wooden walkway above them. About twenty feet away was a perpendicular ladder attached to the side of the dock. Keeping one hand under the struggling woman's chin, Sonny sidekicked toward the dock.

What seemed like hours later, but in reality had probably only been a minute or two, he reached the ladder and shoved the woman toward it. "Grab on!"

She apparently understood because her hand flew out, clawing the air in front of her, missing the side rail by several inches, her movements stiff and clumsy with cold.

Sonny's arms ached, his lungs felt like they might burst. "Grab the ladder!"

She tried again and this time her hand made contact with a rung and her blue-knuckled fingers wrapped around it. Her other hand grabbed hold and she tried to pull herself up while water gushed from her clothes. Her movements were slow and lethargic. She finally quit trying and simply clung to the ladder.

Hypothermia?

Sonny pulled himself up behind her, his legs on either side of hers, his chest pressed against her back. He grasped the ladder with his left hand. With his right, he pried her hand free of the rung and placed it up to the next one. He did the same with her left hand so that both her arms were above her.

"Come on," he gasped against her icy cheek. "Pull."

She pulled.

"Good girl," he praised, his right hand on her waist, urging her higher. "Now your foot. There you go."

Below the sound of the crashing water, he could hear her shallow, labored breathing, close to his ear. He could feel the frailness of her body beneath the layers of heavy, sodden clothes.

They finally gained the last rung, heaved themselves over the top to collapse on the walkway. Wind cut like tiny razors across Sonny's wet skin. His chest burned as he sucked air into his warm lungs, exhaling in a blast of vapor. Salt water stung his eyes. Cold steam, created by the frigid water reacting with the warmer air, rose from both their clothes.

The woman curled to a sitting position, wet hair tangled around her, head bent, coughing, a lake of icy water forming around her. She stopped coughing, but her teeth were chattering. From where he sat, he could see the tremors running through her.

With one shaking hand she pushed the strands of hair back from a semi-transparent cheek, with the other she clutched her heavy sweater to her chest, as if it could give her warmth. Slowly, she turned her face in his direction.

Sonny found himself staring into the bluest, clearest, most unearthly pair of eyes he'd ever seen. Water clung from thick lash tips. Then, one by one, a few shimmering crystal droplets chose to let go and run down her pale cheeks.

He was used to being stared at, but she was looking at him so strangely, her beautiful eyes wide, her lips parted. He felt that she was not only memorizing his face, but looking deep into his very soul.

The person before him seemed ethereal. She was a fog over the lochs, a dew-laden meadow kissed by moonlight. He had the strangest fear that if he touched her again, she might turn to mist.

Another half-formed idea joined the bombardment of his already stunned senses. "Are you a mermaid?" he asked.

Amusement lit her wonderful eyes. She shook her head—an almost imperceptible movement. She let go of the sweater and extended a delicate, blue-veined hand toward him. "Tha-a-nk y-you." The acknowledgment was forced through frozen lips.

In the back of his mind, he knew he had to get her to shelter. But he couldn't seem to move. Beguiled, he could only grasp her icy hand and pray that she wouldn't vanish.

Chapter Two

So cold...

Freezing!

Emily's teeth chattered as shudder after violent shudder wracked her body.

But then, as she stared spellbound at the man beside her, she began to feel mentally removed from the agony of her physical self.

Sonny Maxwell.

The Sonny Maxwell.

It didn't seem possible, but he was even more beautiful in person. His complexion was lighter than the ruddy fishermen she was used to. His lips were a little full—most women would probably call them sexy, their perfect shape accentuated by a golden brown dusting of a two- or three-day beard. She remembered feeling it rub her cheek when he helped her up the ladder.

Even with the water droplets clinging to eyelashes and chin, dripping down the wet strands of hair falling over his collar, he was handsome.

His eyes. She'd never seen eyes that color. They seemed to reflect the clouds, the stormy gray sea.

But it wasn't just his looks that so mesmerized her: it was the soft glow of light she could sense shimmering around him like a force field.

White, with a hint of gray... The color confused her. A person like Sonny Maxwell couldn't have such an aura.

His hand was still grasping hers. She looked down. Beneath his fingertips, where their skin touched, was a warm lavender glow.

How odd. Lavender. The color of humanity...

Dazed, confused, she looked up from their joined hands, back to his eyes. "You...you're white," she said, forcing the words through frozen lips. A gust of wind cut through her and she shivered even more violently.

His eyes, eyes that had been looking at her as if he were a little stunned himself, narrowed with concern. "You're blue. And getting bluer."

Words were forced out through tremors. "You c-can s-see auras t-too?"

Greta had told her that not many men could see auras. They didn't have the sensitivity.

"Auras?" A shiver shook his shoulders. He muttered something about hypothermia and signs of delirium, then shoved himself to his feet, extending a hand toward her. "Come on. We've got to get moving."

Would she be able to stand? Her muscles were cramping. She raised her hand and he pulled her up beside him. As soon as he released her, she wrapped her arms around herself in a futile effort to conduct some heat.

He walked to the other side of the wharf and picked up his leather jacket. When he returned, he tried to put it around her.

"Th-the water—" she protested, barely able to form the words through her numb lips, "w-will ruin it."

He draped it around her shoulders anyway, then held it in place with his arm, her body pressed to his.

The pier stretched out before them, a planked walkway that suddenly looked much longer than it ever had before.

They began walking.

Emily's feet felt like lead, her joints and muscles pulling tighter and tighter.

They walked.

Shaking, teeth chattering… Pain. Her skin hurt, her body hurt, her hands, her feet—

Wind cut through her like a knife.

They walked.

She kept her chin down and her eyes half-closed to protect them from the slicing wind. Her breath rasped in her chest. Beside her, she could hear his labored breathing, see it making a steam cloud before him.

But it didn't seem like they were moving at all. Like a bad dream, she was placing one foot in front of the other, but was getting nowhere. She lifted her head to check on their progress, the wind stinging her eyes. The end of the wharf seemed no closer.

Had to get warm, had to get inside....

In her mind, she pictured a roaring fire. Desperately, she tried to feel its warmth, but failed.

Another series of tremors hit her, coming right on top of the other. Beside her, Sonny Maxwell was shaking almost as badly.

"Come on, Emily. You can't stop now."

She managed some more steps, vaguely wondering how he knew her name. Of course, everybody knew *his* name.

Sonny Maxwell.

Sonny Maxwell to the rescue...to the rescue...to the rescue....

From a distance came a voice, raised in alarm, penetrating her fog-enshrouded brain. She heard footsteps hammering over wooden planks.

"Emily!"

It was Annie McEntire, the postmistress. Her voice cut through the pain-induced haze. "Emily! You poor, poor dear! We have to get you home immediately!"

Emily sensed rather than felt Annie pat her hand. She experienced a moment of panic when she was pulled from Sonny's grasp, his arm replaced by Annie's.

"Come on, honey," Annie coaxed.

Emily lifted her face, searching behind her, wind burning her cheeks. Sonny Maxwell was gone. And she hadn't even thanked him.

Annie took charge. Emily wasn't aware of walking up the hill to her house, but suddenly they were inside the door, being bombarded by a stream of questions from her three younger sisters.

"Emily will tell you later," Annie said, shooing the girls away.

She helped Emily out of her clothes and into a tepid bath, increasing the water temperature as Emily's body thawed.

"You're lucky to be alive," she said, clucking her tongue.

"And imagine—to be pulled out of the water by *Sonny Maxwell*, of all people." Her voice was a combination of awe and disgust.

The whole island had been humming about Sonny Maxwell for weeks, ever since he'd made reservations at the St. Genevieve Inn. And even though there was no theater on the island, they had magazines, radio, television and VCRs. Sonny Maxwell's face was as well-known as the President's. More so, maybe.

"Paid to look pretty," Annie said. "Imagine that. What kind of world are we living in where a person can make a living by looking pretty? It's sinful."

A week ago Emily's father had said much the same thing, and Emily had agreed. But that was before she'd come face to face with Sonny Maxwell.

There weren't many people Emily disliked—no one, when she really thought about it. But, upon the occasion they should ever have met, she'd been prepared to dislike Sonny Maxwell. If it was true what the tabloids said, there was hardly a woman in the world who hadn't spent a night in his bed. And anyone who treated women as sex objects, anyone whose life revolved around materialistic pleasure seeking and self-gratification couldn't be anyone she would like.

But that had been before.

He'd been a surprise. Nothing like she'd expected. There had been something about him that had seemed to call to her . . . a sadness, maybe. Or possibly a loneliness. But how could someone like Sonny Maxwell be lonely?

"And with your father out to sea," Annie said, chattering away, "it would be the end of the poor man if he lost you, too. I've never seen a man take a death any harder than he took your mother's. I told him he shouldn't have planted that weeping willow tree. Somebody always dies after a person plants a weeping willow tree."

By the time Emily was dry and tucked in bed with a hot water bottle and a bowl of soup, she was feeling almost herself. But what about Sonny Maxwell? He'd been just as wet, just as cold. Had someone fixed hot soup for him? Or tucked a hot water bottle at his feet? And she hadn't even thanked him, hadn't even offered her home and fire.

"Now you just rest," Annie said. "I'll get the girls' supper."

"You've done enough, Annie. Claire is twelve. She can get supper on the table."

"I won't hear of it. I won't go home until I know everything here is in order."

In another hour and a half Annie was gone, leaving Emily feeling guilty for the relief she felt at the peace that had descended.

She let out a sigh and stared down at the quilt that covered her. The swatches of fabric represented different family members: a piece of her mother's apron, a blouse that had belonged to Claire, a dress of Tilly's, a jumper of little Babbie's, denim from Papa's jeans.

She touched a finger to a patch of light blue calico. It was from the dress she'd worn the first day of school. Emily remembered her mother holding the bolt of cloth to her small chin, declaring that the cornflower blue perfectly matched her eyes.

But their family was shattered when Sara Christian died of a misdiagnosed ruptured appendix. The doctor had said it was just a bad case of the flu. Now, Emily's mother lay in a grave on the hillside overlooking the harbor.

She had been gone four years. It didn't hurt as much to think of her now. The pain was tempered with bittersweet memories. But Christmas and birthdays—special times were still hard to get through.

A small sound from the vicinity of the bedroom door, like that of a tiny mouse, drew Emily from her reflections. The door creaked and swung open, inch by slow inch. Five-year-old Babbie stuck her head inside. "Emily...?"

"Come on in, sweetheart."

"Annie said to leave you alone."

Emily patted the bed. "I could really use some company."

Babbie came in, followed by twelve-year-old Claire and ten-year-old Tilly. Unlike Emily, who was a throwback of her grandmother's Swedish ancestry, all three girls reflected their father's strong Irish heritage. Their eyes were green, their hair dark brown.

Babbie scrambled up on the bed and cuddled next to Emily. Her little sister smelled like soap and bleach and clothes that had been dried outside.

"Tell us about the prince who rescued you," she begged.

Tilly let out a loud snort. "He wasn't a prince. His name is Sonny Maxwell. He's an actor and a model, not a prince."

"I can call him a prince, can't I, Emily?"

"How about calling him the make-out king," Tilly mumbled under her breath.

"Tilly—" Emily frowned. Tilly spent far too much time in front of the television. Even though she wasn't supposed to watch soap operas and tabloid TV, Emily had caught her at it more than once.

Emily patted Babbie's leg. "You can call him a prince if you want."

"I can't believe you met Sonny Maxwell," Claire said. She came around the side of the bed, picked up a comb and began running it through Emily's damp blond tresses. "What was he like? What did he say?"

"What color were his eyes?" Babbie wanted to know.

"Gray," Claire said.

"How do you know?" Babbie asked.

"I saw it in a magazine."

"Did he ride a noble steed?" Babbie's words came out in a breathless rush.

Tilly rolled her eyes.

Emily pulled Babbie close and ruffled her tumbling dark curls. "No, sweetheart. I'm sorry. There was not a noble steed in sight."

Babbie's face fell, then brightened. "Maybe it was waiting behind a building."

Tilly leaned close to Claire and whispered, "More like a big black Harley with a babe on back."

"Tilly!"

Middle child syndrome, Emily had to remind herself. She'd read all about it. Claire was so polite and poised that it seemed Tilly went out of her way to be the very opposite. Claire was a model student, while Tilly was always having to stay after school. She constantly tried to be the center of attention by doing and saying outrageous things.

"Come on, Tilly. Sit down and listen to the story."

"Okay." Trying to act as if she wasn't really interested, Tilly shuffled across the room, crossed her arms at her waist and plopped down on the bed, her legs dangling over the rail.

"The story, Emily," Claire begged.

Emily laughed. "Okay, okay. Now stop shaking the bed!"

They settled down, their faces expectant, even Tilly's. Never had Emily had such a rapt audience.

"As you know, I was bringing in the kite, just like I always do—"

"The dragon kite?" Babbie interrupted.

For over a year Emily had been trying to perfect the dragon design. Now, reminded of the loss of her gangling, ungraceful creation, she smiled a little wistfully and said, "Yes, the dragon kite."

"I knew it. It *had* to be the dragon," Babbie said. "The prince rescues her from the dragon."

"Let Emily tell it," Claire said.

Emily told them of how the kite had been wrenched by the wind, how she had grabbed for it and had fallen into the frigid waters. How she'd been pulled beneath the surface and darkness had filled her. How she'd felt as if death might be very close....

But then Sonny Maxwell had come.

And she had felt his white-and-gray light stronger than she'd ever felt anyone's light before.

As a small child, Emily had discovered that in times of high emotion or stress, certain people put off a light she could sense.

The islanders said it was because she was a December's child, born between the hours of midnight and dawn of Christmas Day. Emily wasn't sure what she believed, she only knew she could sometimes sense colors.

The only other person she knew of who had the same strange ability was Greta Svenson, the midwife who lived on the other side of the island. Greta had told her that the light was called an aura, and that it was a reflection of a person's heart and soul.

She'd also told her that a white aura was a sign of purity and goodness. Gray was the color of pain and sadness. Of emptiness. It was the color sometimes seen when a person dies, when the soul leaves the body.

Purity and emptiness.

That's what Sonny Maxwell's aura had been telling her.

"What did he say when he pulled you from the water?" Claire asked, her voice breathless in anticipation, interrupting Emily's confused musings, pulling her thoughts back to the present.

Emily drew her blanket-draped legs closer to her, wrapping her arms around her knees. "He asked me if I was a mermaid."

That got the gasp she'd hoped for.

"Did you get his autograph?" Claire asked.

"Oh, *I'm sure!*" Tilly said. "They were both freezing to death!"

"I'd love to have his autograph," Claire said sighing.

"Hey, I know. Let's invite him to dinner," Tilly suggested.

They all looked at her. Claire started jumping up and down, clapping her hands. "Yes, let's! Let's!"

Emily frowned.

"Please, oh please," they all three begged.

"To thank him," Claire added.

"Well..." Emily shot Tilly a severe look. "If Tilly can behave...."

"Cross my heart." Tilly drew an *X* on her chest and smiled a smile that made Emily want to hug her and scold her at the same time.

"Oh, sure," Claire said, rolling her eyes and mimicking her sister. "You can't be good for a whole evening."

"Wanna bet?" Tilly demanded.

"Girls!" Emily broke in. "Of course Tilly can be good. Can't you, Tilly?"

"Sure."

Emily wanted to believe her. Oh, how she wanted to believe her.

Chapter Three

Sonny was standing in the second-floor bedroom of the St. Genevieve Inn, getting ready to head to Emily Christian's house. He'd asked the tomboy who'd returned his jacket a few casually placed questions and found out that Emily's mother was dead and Emily was helping to raise three younger sisters, one being the ornery-looking Tilly Christian.

His first instinct had been to decline the dinner invitation. He wasn't a mingler, never had been. And it was too late to start now. But he couldn't get Emily Christian out of his head. No matter what he was doing, or where he was, he kept reenacting the events of yesterday. And the main point of his focus dwelt upon that slow-motion moment when he'd looked Emily Christian full in the face and felt the earth move.

Corny? No doubt.

He couldn't figure it out, but he knew there had to be a logical explanation. His own borderline hypothermia, maybe.

He grabbed his shirt from the bed and shrugged into it, tucked in the tail, buttoned and zipped his jeans. Then he raked his fingers through his straight hair, giving his reflection a cursory glance in the cloudy oval mirror hanging above the ornate dresser.

Doreen was right. He needed a haircut.

He'd no sooner thought about her complaint about his hair, when a rapid, no-nonsense knock sounded at the door.

Doreen.

She had a distinctive knock.

He opened the door to find her standing in the hallway, a hand on her hip, the big tan purse she always carried slung over one shoulder.

Her eyes took in his white oxford shirt and clean jeans. "So," she said, disapproval in her voice and stance. "You're going."

"Yeah."

They had known each other so long that Doreen assumed she had the right to gripe about the way he lived. Maybe she did.

"You were an idiot to jump in that water yesterday," she said.

"I'm a strong swimmer."

An understatement. He could have elaborated, but he didn't. He rarely elaborated on anything.

"What if you get sick from your little swim?" Doreen asked. "They probably don't even have a doctor on this island." She snorted. "But then maybe that's all for the best. If they did, he'd probably burn roots shaped like men, chant incantations and use leeches."

"Come on, Doreen," Sonny said, wishing she'd lighten up. "You're not up on things. Medical schools are back to using leeches. And you don't have anything to worry about," he added. "I *never* get sick. You know that."

She made an impatient sound with her tongue. "You know what I mean. These people aren't like us. They're frozen in time."

"It amazes me how a nice person like you can be so damned narrow-minded." Sonny scooped up his room key from the dresser, pocketed it, then shrugged into his jacket.

Leaning against the wall next to the door was Emily Christian's tattered dragon kite. When Sonny had gone back to the wharf to get his boots, he'd fished the kite from the water. Now he tucked the dry, broken remnants under his arm and stepped into the hallway with Doreen, shutting the door behind him.

"It's called being realistic," she said. "Normally I'd be thrilled at seeing you take an interest in something that's going on around you. But Sonny—" The worry lines in her face deepened. "Not *these* people."

"Why not these people? You're the last person I would have expected to be prejudiced."

"I'm not prejudiced. I'll even grudgingly admit that the islanders have a certain charm. I just don't want to see you get involved in something that will be hard to get out of.''

"Doreen, we're talking about dinner, not marriage. You're reading stuff into this that isn't there.''

She let out a deep breath and shook her head. "You're probably right. Guess maybe I'm going a little stir crazy or something. Doting in my old age.''

"Don't get started on that old age stuff. You're the youngest fifty-seven-year-old I know.''

"That's funny. You're the oldest twenty-eight-year-old *I* know.''

He gave her his usual reply. "Go to hell, Doreen.''

It was a standing joke between them. Seven years ago she'd wanted to photograph him. He'd told her no, but she'd persisted. She had followed him, called, hadn't given up, not even when he told her to go to hell. So he'd finally said yes, just to get rid of her. His career had been moderately successful up until that point. It had taken Doreen and her skill with a camera to make him famous.

Now, every so often, just for old time's sake, he told her to go to hell.

She walked him to the top of the steps. "Don't stay out too late. We need to be up by four to catch that pure light. Hopefully we'll be able to wrap up in one more day and get the hell out of here.''

Like a kid facing a return to school after summer vacation, Sonny felt a flutter of panic at the thought of going back to neon and concrete. He wished the vacation could last forever. Like an adult, he knew that was impossible.

*   *   *

Fog swirled about his feet as he followed the winding lane that led to the gray two-story house perched atop the hill like some moody painting.

For a second Sonny wished he'd brought along his camera. It would have made a great picture. The house silhouetted against the darkening sky, the fog, everything in shades of gray. Lonely. Mysterious. A little magical. Just the right place for a mermaid to live.

As he approached, smells of wood smoke mingled with the briny scent of the ocean, the smell of the damp earth under foot. Warm light poured from the latticed windows, reaching out to him across the uneven walk. He wasn't sure which door to use—front or back. He finally settled on the front one that opened onto the porch.

He climbed steps that had been painted a gray enamel, and knocked.

From behind the door he heard excited voices followed by running feet. The door opened wide and he was greeted by three dark-haired girls. He wasn't too good at figuring kids' ages. He guessed one to be about twelve or thirteen, the youngest five or six.

He'd seen the middle one before. She'd brought back his jacket. Dressed in jeans and a baggy sweatshirt, hair tied in a ponytail, she looked more . . . he wanted to say American, but they were all Americans.

It was a little unnerving the way they were all staring up at him, eyes wide.

"Hi," he offered.

"Hi." All three spoke in unison.

"Emily!" the middle girl shrieked, never taking her eyes off Sonny. "He's here!"

From behind the girls, footsteps sounded on the wooden floor. He looked past the sea of dark hair and green eyes to find Emily Christian standing there, hands clasped in front of her.

"Please—come in."

Her voice was low and soothing, like the brook that ran behind his cabin in the woods.

He stepped across the threshold—into Emily Christian's world.

It was a warm world with waxed wood floors and ruffled curtains at the windows. At one end of the living room stood a black-and-silver woodstove. Most of the furniture looked antique. If not for the incongruity of the TV, stereo and telephone, he could almost think he'd stepped back in time.

Emily was wearing a print dress along with dark stockings and brown leather shoes. Her blond hair was braided, hanging to her waist. Fine tiny curls had escaped around her hairline, framing her delicate features.

Most of the women he was around were models; he wasn't used to seeing a face so free of makeup as Emily's. Her skin was light and smooth, her cheeks glowed.

She was just as beautiful as he'd remembered. Just as otherworldly as he'd remembered.

And her eyes. God, her eyes. They were so blue. When he looked into them, he felt the same strange pull he'd felt out there on the wharf. He had the uncanny sensation that she could read his mind, see into his heart and soul, his past and future. Which was crazy.

At the same time he sensed an inexplicable danger. He felt that in some strange way, she had the power to hurt him.

He shouldn't have come.

But he was careful to keep his trepidation from showing. He was good at that, at putting up a front, at keeping his inner self hidden.

Then he noticed that she was staring at his left side, curiosity in her eyes. He remembered the kite and held it out to her. "I'm sorry. There's not much of it left."

She took it and held it in her arms, her fingers smoothing the emerald fabric. "It's my fault. The design is unstable. I've tried lighter material, different struts—" She made a small, sad sound, then put the ruined kite aside on a nearby bench. When she turned back, she was once again the hostess. "May I take your coat?"

He shrugged out of his leather flight jacket, all the while aware that the children were still staring. The oldest girl's eyes were full of adoration—which he was used to, the middle child, Tilly's eyes were bland, completely unimpressed, bored almost. He liked that. And the youngest . . .

She reached up and shyly touched her fingers to the back of his hand, a butterfly skimming his knuckles. "Did you ride your noble steed?" she asked.

Steed? He'd seen a few horses on the island.... He cast a helpless glance over his shoulder.

Tilly put a hand to her mouth and ribbed the older girl with an elbow. "Babbie thinks you're a prince," she explained.

Babbie continued to stare up at him, her eyes huge and trusting. "Tilly said you're not a prince, you're a king. King of—"

Whatever she was going to say was lost as Emily clapped her hands. "Girls! Girls! I think you'd better go to the kitchen and set the table. Claire—" Hands to young shoulders, Emily ushered them in the direction of the kitchen.

Claire shuffled along, head turned, eyes dreamy, catching a final look.

"Good grief! He's not *that* cute," he heard Tilly say as she gave her sister a final push through the kitchen door. "It's not like he's a hockey player or something."

Emily turned to Sonny, frown lines between her brows. "I'm terribly sorry. Tilly is very outspoken."

"That's okay. It's good for me. Keeps my ego in line." He handed her his jacket, suddenly uncomfortably aware of the designer label sewn on the inside collar, of the rich suppleness of the leather. A cashy item.

When she took it from him, he saw that her fragile hand trembled. It wasn't evident in her face or voice, but now he knew she was just as nervous as he was.

The difference was, she belonged here, he didn't.

A heavy footfall sounded on the stairs.

Emily looked up. "Papa, come and meet Sonny Maxwell."

Then Sonny's hand was being crushed by John Christian's.

"I want to thank you for saving my daughter's life," the burly man said while continuing to pump Sonny's hand. "If I'd 'uv lost my Emily—" His voice caught and he couldn't continue.

Emily came to the rescue. "I'm alive and well." She flashed Sonny one of the sweetest smiles he believed he'd ever seen, then she was leading them both to the kitchen, in the direction of those good smells.

There had only been a couple of times when Sonny had eaten a meal with a family. He usually ate fast food or restaurant food, or, when he was alone at his cabin, he'd just heat something from out of a can— when he remembered to eat at all.

Sonny took a seat at one end of the table, John Christian at the other. To his left were Claire and Babbie, his right, Tilly and Emily.

He wasn't used to saying prayers, either. Seeing all the bowed heads, he awkwardly locked his fingers together.

John Christian said the blessing. "Thank You, Lord, for this food which Emily has worked so hard to prepare. And thank You for sending a stranger into our midst to pull my daughter from the sea."

Amens were heard all around the table.

The meal consisted of fish chowder loaded with potatoes and carrots, hot homemade bread with butter, and blackberry jam. It was some of the best food Sonny had ever tasted.

He'd never been good at small talk, but somehow the warmth of the small kitchen sneaked up on him. Or maybe it was the soft smiles Emily would occasionally send his way. Whatever the reason, he began to relax.

Claire even came out of the clouds enough to ask, "How old were you when you made your first commercial?"

"About four. Younger than Babbie."

"Did you like it?" Tilly asked.

He thought a moment. "It was fun, like playing pretend."

More importantly, it had made his mother happy. But she never stayed happy long. One moment, she would hug and kiss him, the next she would shove him away. He'd been too young to understand that her violent mood swings were due to alcoholism.

"That sounds really neat," Tilly said. "I heard about a kid who was making a movie, and he didn't have to go to school. Did you ever get to ditch school?"

"If I missed very much school, a tutor would come to the studio and work with me."

"That would be so neat!" Claire and Tilly said in unison.

He didn't want them to get the wrong idea, didn't want them to think that his life had been fuller than theirs. Nothing was further from the truth.

And he didn't like to talk about his childhood, didn't even like to think about it. He'd been seven when he learned that being a child actor wasn't so neat. He'd wanted to go to a birthday party, but his mother made him go for an audition instead. Once there, he'd sulked and refused to say his lines correctly and some other kid ended up getting the part.

His mother went berserk. He'd seen her mad, but never like this. She jerked him out of the studio, shoved him into the convertible one of her men friends had bought for her, drove him home and told him to pack all of his things.

The next day she took him to a huge four-story mansion—surrounded by a black iron fence—a boardinghouse for child actors, the place that was to be his home for the next several years.

"I'd like to be on TV and miss school," Tilly said.

"It wasn't as great as it sounds," Sonny told her. "There weren't many other kids around, and it was pretty boring most of the time. You had to be ready for your part, even if it meant waiting all day to say one line. It wasn't so great," he repeated.

He looked up to find Emily staring at him, her eyes huge and sad, full of question and a strange compassion. Again he had the uncanny feeling that she could read his mind.

Then her eyes pulled away from his. "Well, who's ready for pie," she asked.

"What I think is neat," Tilly said, "is the way you get paid for doing nothing."

"Tilly—" John Christian cut in from the end of the table. "Help Emily with dessert."

Tilly was half out of her seat when she paused and said, "Emily and Papa say it's sinful for a person to get paid for his looks, but I think it's neat."

In half a heartbeat a heavy silence descended.

Sonny felt as if he'd been kicked in the stomach. Their opinion of him shouldn't matter. He knew that. But for some reason it did.

It was always the same. He would find something, only to have it taken away, only to find out it hadn't been real to begin with.

At age ten, he'd been pulled off the set to be told that his mother had been discovered dead in a hotel room.

He'd felt like somebody had kicked him in the stomach then, too.

But the shoot had continued. The show must go on.

Later, he'd overheard one of the light technicians talking about what a heartless little bastard he was. At the time, Sonny had wanted to tell them he was just doing what he'd been taught to do. Pretend.

It not only came in handy in front of the camera, but in real life.

Like now. He had sensed danger here. His instincts had been right.

He pushed his chair away and got to his feet.

"Sonny—"

Emily was coming around the table toward him, her face creased with concern and embarrassment, and something he didn't want to see: pity.

He was careful to keep his expression neutral, his voice polite. ''Thanks for the meal. I'll pass on dessert.''

Mechanically he brushed past her, through the living room. He wrenched open the front door, the damp night air hitting him full in the face. He pulled in a deep breath, stepped out and shut the door behind him.

Emily stood staring at the closed door, Sonny's frozen face an image in her mind.

His jacket still hung from the wooden peg near the door. She snatched it from the hook and hurried outside.

A low-lying fog had moved in, but the light from the windows illuminated the area around the house. She could see him just past the edge of light, a darker shadow among the shadows. He'd already reached the end of the sidewalk and was ready to walk down the lane that led to the main road.

''Sonny! Wait!''

He stopped and turned and waited for her.

What on earth could she say to rectify what had happened? Nothing.

When she caught up with him, she handed him the jacket. Emily knew it was her fault, not Tilly's. The child was only repeating what Emily had said not a week ago.

Emily reached for Sonny, but stopped before her fingers could touch him—an imploring gesture, begging his pardon for the unpardonable. "I'm so sorry...."

"It's okay. I'm used to it." His voice was neutral, sterile and polite. "Forget about it. Go back to the house. It's cold out here."

"I did say those awful things, I can't deny it."

"Everybody has an opinion."

"Yes, but that was before I met you."

"That shouldn't make any difference. I'm the same person I was a week ago."

Oh, Lord. A sob rose in her throat. She clenched and unclenched her hands. "You saved my life! I'm so ashamed of myself. I never thought I was one to judge somebody on gossip before meeting them. I was wrong."

"No, you were right. Absolutely right."

Someone else may not have been able to detect it, but Emily could hear the pain that crept around the neutral edges of his voice. And it hurt her to know she'd hurt him.

Oh, Sonny. I'm so sorry.

A damp breeze curled around her legs, tugging her skirt, whipping it against her legs.

There was nothing she could say, nothing she could do. So she did nothing, said nothing.

He reached out and touched her very lightly on the cheek, the pads of his fingers barely skimming her skin. And in that touch she sensed regret—like someone who touches something they know they can never have. "You're crying," he whispered with a sort of bewildered awe. His voice was so deep that it seemed she could actually feel it vibrating in her chest, around the ache she felt in her heart.

"Don't cry, Emily."

"I'm not." She denied it, even though she knew it was true. All her life she'd cried other people's tears.

"You *are* crying."

He wiped a tear from her face, then draped his jacket around her shoulders. She reached up and grasped the collar, hugging it to her.

She felt rather than saw his eyes probing the darkness as he stared down at her, his warm hands on her arms. His next words took her by surprise.

"Are you real?" he whispered.

"I'm very real."

"You feel real."

"I'm real."

Her heart was hammering. Her tears were forgotten. She thought about how his lips would feel, pressed to hers, and she suddenly felt dizzy.

His hands left her, and for a brief second fear stabbed through her. She was afraid he was leaving. But he lifted one of her hands, bent his head and pressed his mouth to her open palm.

When he let go, she curled her fingers, cupping the imprint of his kiss in her hand. She would keep it, she would save it forever. Sonny Maxwell's kiss.

"How old are you?" he asked.

"Twenty."

"So young."

"Not so young." She would have asked his age, but there was no need. She already knew that he was twenty-eight.

He ran a finger along her jaw. Slowly. Drowsily...

"Have you ever been kissed?" he whispered, his words scaring and thrilling her at the same time.

She'd been kissed many times. By her sisters, aunts, her father, cousins. She'd even had a few dates, but the boys on St. Genevieve were in the market for brides, and she hadn't been interested.

"*Really* kissed?" he whispered.

Things had turned. Earlier, she had control, but she'd since lost it. She was now in unfamiliar waters. "I'm not sure...." she said.

"Not sure?"

She sensed that he smiled. She could tell by his voice that he didn't believe her.

"You've been—" she couldn't believe she was asking this "—you've been kissed...a lot?"

"Not so many times. And never by a mermaid."

"Oh." What else was there to say?

He pulled her close against the warmth of his chest. She felt his hand cup her chin, tilting her face up while he lowered his to her.

Her lips parted in anticipation.

Her reaction was instantaneous. When his mouth touched hers, a languid heat crept through her veins, making her feel as if she'd drunk too much of Greta Svenson's special cough medicine. She clung to his shoulders.

His lips were soft and gentle and full of tender reverence. She pressed herself closer, so close she could feel the hard, sinewy lines of his body, feel his warm, steady heartbeat beneath her breasts.

A shudder coursed through him. His mouth caressed hers one last time, then pulled away.

He took a deep breath. To Emily, the sound made her think of someone pulling himself together after a near collision.

"There. Now I've been kissed by a mermaid," he said.

She could only smile, a little dazed.

"Goodbye, Emily Christian."

"Goodbye."

He turned and disappeared into the mist.

"Thank you for saving my life, Sonny Maxwell," she whispered, her eyes blurring with tears, her throat aching.

Long after he'd gone, she stared and stared into the darkness. In her cupped palm and on her lips, she felt the imprint of his kiss. She was still staring into the mist when, only half-aware, she heard a door slam, then her father was beside her, laying a hand on her shoulder.

Emily couldn't ever remember a time when her father hadn't been there for her. As a child, her lungs had been weak and she hadn't been as robust as the other children. When she was sick, her father would sit beside her bed and read to her, or carve figures out of driftwood.

"I'm sorry, Emily."

The Irish lilt that always crept into his voice during times of stress and high emotion was there now. "God knows, I'll be forever grateful he was there to pull you from the water."

It wasn't until then that Emily realized she was still wearing Sonny's jacket. She hugged it to her. "I've done a great wrong," she said. "I prejudged someone I had no right to judge and my own spiteful words came back at me. A man's worth shouldn't be measured by how much weight he can lift, or how many loads of wood he hauls in a day, or how fast he can row against the wind."

"I know, sweetheart. But you didn't mean it." The arm around her tightened. "Come in before you get sick. But I'll have to warn you, the house is not a happy place to be right now. All three girls are yowling to raise the roof. Tilly because of what she said, Claire because she didn't get the young man's autograph, and Babbie because Tilly scared her prince away."

For some reason, his words made her think of the fairy tale of Beauty and the Beast. No one could see past the beast's outer shell. Even though Sonny was beautiful, it seemed he had the same problem. And she wondered if anyone would ever see the man within.

Chapter Four

Emily sat in the dimly lit kite shop, head bent over the humming sewing machine. With a boot toe pressed to the foot pedal, she fed in red satin, folding the fabric as she went, making the dowel casing for the kite.

Her kite-making mail order enterprise had begun as a labor of love, but had quickly grown into a thriving business—more business than she could handle. Rather than expand she had chosen to turn down orders—which only seemed to make more of a demand for her creations.

She couldn't remember a time when she hadn't been fascinated by kites. When she was a child her father would take her out in his fishing boat on lazy Sunday afternoons. She'd tie a string to the bow and fly the kite high above the ocean. But the ocean winds usually proved too strong for the delicate store-bought kites, so Emily began making them herself. Instead of using paper, she used cloth. And instead of string, she used fishing line.

The first kites she made were traditional diamond-shape. Later, she tried more imaginative and daring designs.

So far, the dragon kite she'd lost the day she'd fallen from the wharf was her biggest and most elaborate undertaking.

Memories of that day just naturally brought with it thoughts of Sonny Maxwell. She'd tried but she couldn't quit thinking about him. There had been something in him, in his eyes that seemed to reach out for something in her.

She came to the end of the fabric, took her foot from the treadle, cut the thread and shut off the machine. Then she stretched, straightening her spine and rubbing her lower back. Every muscle in her body ached, her eyes burned, and she'd had a headache all day. She wondered if she was coming down with something.

She got up and went to the cramped back room that served as a makeshift kitchen. The clock on the wall read four forty-five. Four hours since she'd taken any aspirin. In fifteen more minutes she could lock up, but her day wouldn't be over. She had an order to finish for a specialty store in Bangor, Maine. She'd promised to have a dozen kites in the mail by tomorrow and she'd never been late with an order before. She wasn't going to be late with this one—not even if it meant staying up all night.

She filled a glass from the faucet and washed down two more aspirin. It hurt her throat to swallow.

She couldn't afford to be sick. Not now.

It was no one's fault but her own. She would have been done with the Bangor order by now if she hadn't allowed herself to be distracted. Numerous times—too many to count—she'd found herself staring blankly out the window, thinking about a pair of stormy eyes, a pair of strong arms, a pair of warm, warm lips....

When Sonny had held her against his heart, when he'd pressed his lips to hers while the ocean roared and the night mist whirled around them, it had felt so right. So wonderful. If only...

The clock struck five, bringing her out of another daydream. Feeling a little irritated with her lack of self-control, she went to the front of the store and turned the Closed sign around. Through the glass she could see the purple unicorn she'd put out this morning. It was still flying high above the gray ocean. She sighed, wondering if summer would ever come, wondering if the sun had forgotten their tiny island.

She went down to the pier and brought in the kite. Then before locking up, she looked outside to make sure no late customer was hurrying in the direction of her shop. The wooden walkway was deserted. She closed the heavy door, a gust of wind curling about her ankles, creeping up her woolen skirt.

Her eyes were drawn to the leather jacket that hung over the ladder-back chair. For the past two days she'd watched for Sonny, hoping he'd stop in looking for his jacket, but he hadn't. And now she heard he was leaving. During the off-season the ferryboat came to St. Genevieve once a week, on Saturdays—and tomorrow was Saturday.

Tomorrow he would be gone.

Coming to a decision, Emily lifted the jacket from the wooden spindles of the chairback, took the key from the hook near the counter and left the shop, locking the door behind her.

It wasn't until she stepped into the lobby of the inn that she realized she'd have to ask for Sonny's room number. And Kelly McFarlin was working the desk. Kelly was two years older than Emily and had a brood of four quite incorrigible little children, with another on the way. And nine times out of ten Kelly was the direct source of most gossip heard around St. Genevieve.

Emily had known better than to come here. Good women didn't go to men's hotel rooms. Maybe she should leave the coat with Kelly.

No.

She took a deep breath and marched up to the desk.

"Emily! What a surprise!" Kelly said.

She looked even more surprised when Emily asked for Sonny's room number. As soon as the number left Kelly's slyly smiling lips, Emily spun around and headed for the stairs, aware of the pair of curious and speculative eyes on her back.

When she reached the second-story landing, a wave of dizziness washed over her. She paused, a steadying hand on the wooden railing. The peculiar feeling passed almost as soon as it had come. Blaming it on nerves she moved down the hallway. When she reached Sonny's room she raised her hand preparing to knock but found herself unable to do so. Instead she had to fight the urge to hang his coat on the doorknob and run.

But she forced her frozen arm to move, forced her knuckles to rap against the door. Then she stepped back and waited, the jacket gripped tightly in front of her.

She shouldn't have come...shouldn't have come....

The doorknob turned. The door opened. And then Sonny was standing in the doorway, barefoot, dressed in a white T-shirt and gray sweatpants. His sun-bleached hair was tousled. His eyes looked a little sleepy, as if he'd been resting, or sleeping, or—

Oh my.

She couldn't help but think of some of the stories she'd read. Women went crazy over him. They attacked him, they craved him. They brazenly chased him, they waited in his bed for him.

Emily suddenly realized that she probably seemed no different than the millions of other women who wanted to be touched by Sonny Maxwell, who wanted to discover the sexuality his heavy-lidded eyes hinted at.

Heat flooded her cheeks.

He was watching her. Had any of her thoughts been mirrored on her face?

"Here—" Lest he think she'd come for any other reason, she thrust the jacket at him. "You forgot this the other night."

He crossed his arms over his chest and leaned a shoulder against the doorjamb.

"Keep it."

"No, I—"

"Go ahead." He shrugged. "I have another one."

"I couldn't. It's obviously expensive."

An understatement. She could have purchased a new wardrobe for what the jacket must have cost. His languid body language said he was relaxed and at ease. But his eyes... He was watching her with an intensity that took her breath away.

He pushed himself away from the doorjamb, unfurling his arms at the same time. He took a step toward her, then stopped. One hand came up. Then she felt his knuckles lightly skimming her overheated cheek.

And the touch of his hand on her skin seemed... so... *nice*.

"God, you're beautiful," he whispered, the unmistakable longing in his voice surprising her. "Untouched," he said.

His eyes roamed her face, her hair, back to her eyes.

She stood staring up at him. His eyes held secrets and wonderful promises. And his touch made her heart beat faster, louder.

"Lord, how I wish—" His words broke off and his expression changed, hardened a little, as if he'd just remembered who he was and who she was. His hand fell away from her face.

He couldn't stop now! "What do you wish?" she asked, not quite able to keep the desperation from her voice.

"I wish . . ." He smiled a little crookedly, laughing at his own foolishness it seemed, "I wish you were just a little bit bad. No, change that. I wish *I* were a little bit good."

She couldn't believe he'd ever done anything bad. He had called her untouched, but as contradictory as it seemed, untouched was the very word she would have used to describe Sonny. With her, she knew he'd meant untouched in the physical sense. With Sonny it was something more. Something that transcended physical bounds.

"What have you done in your life that could be so terrible?" she asked.

His eyes clouded. She could almost see his thoughts turn inward. "It's what I haven't done."

She hated the sadness in his voice, hated the weariness. As if he'd given up. "You talk as if your life is over," she said.

"Sometimes I feel like it is. Sometimes I'm ready for it to be."

"Don't say that. You're young."

"I'm tired. Tired of playing the game." The expression in his eyes had changed. Now they seemed to reflect the wasteland of his soul. She stared at him, trying to feel what he felt, and became aware of a faint glow around him.

White touched with gray.

His aura *was* white. She thought she'd only imagined it the day he'd pulled her from the water. Darkness had been falling, and she'd been anything but clearheaded.

"You're white," she murmured in puzzled amazement, hardly aware that she spoke the words aloud.

"White?" His eyebrows drew together. "That's what you said on the wharf. What are you talking about?"

The island people were used to her strange gift, some even seeming to accept it as simply a part of the ways of St. Genevieve. But Emily hadn't been very old when she'd learned not to mention it to mainlanders. They didn't understand.

"It's nothing," she said, hating to trivialize something so special, yet unable to face Sonny's scorn.

"Come on. Tell me."

She took a deep breath. "Sometimes...when I concentrate on someone long enough," she said, unable to meet his penetrating gaze, "I see a glow around them. An aura."

"A glow?"

"Well, I'm not sure if I actually *see* it with my eyes. It's more of a feeling."

"And you say my...aura is white?"

"Yes. But white is good," she rushed on to explain. "It symbolizes purity of heart."

He gave her a funny smile, and she could tell he was wondering about her mental state.

"And what color is your aura?" he asked.

"I've never seen my own, but Greta—she's a mid-wife with second sight—she told me it's blue."

"Blue."

"Not light blue and not dark blue but somewhere in between. Blue means..." Well, she could hardly tell him that blue meant she was a loving person. "Blue is a good color, too."

He shook his head. "I've never met anybody like you."

"You don't believe me, do you? About the colors?" She knew he wouldn't. He came from a world where everything was based on reality, on things that could be seen and felt and held in one's hands.

"It doesn't surprise me," he said. "When I first saw you, I thought you were a mermaid...someone magic and mystical."

"I'm real."

"I know." He sighed, then smiled. And the smile held a trace of the longing she'd thought she'd seen earlier, and it also seemed to hold a trace of regret.

He looked down the hallway, past her. "You better run along," he told her. "Before somebody sees you with me."

She suddenly realized she didn't want to tell him goodbye. She would have liked to have gotten to know him better. She would have liked to have made him smile, maybe even make him laugh because she was sure he didn't laugh very often.

But they were worlds apart. She was a fisherman's daughter who made pretty kites. He was famous, a beautiful man who made the world sigh.

She managed to pull forth a brave smile, managed to look directly into his storm-colored eyes.

"Goodbye, Sonny Maxwell." She pressed the jacket into his hands. "Thank you."

He stood there, regarding her with a calm, world-weariness. She wished she could change things, and be the person to plant a bit of hope in his fallow heart.

Since she was the daughter of a fisherman and a child of the sea, she said, "I hope that someday you find a boat that takes you where you want to go."

He smiled a little at that.

Not waiting for an answer where there was none, she turned and hurried away so he wouldn't see her tears.

Sonny watched Emily go. He'd never wanted much in his life, but he suddenly wanted to stop her and ask her to stay a little longer, to talk to him about her magic colors, to lighten his darkness a little more.

But he didn't reach out for people.

If you don't reach out, your hand can't get knocked away.

The day his mother ~~had taken him to the boarding~~-house, he'd cried for her. A woman he'd never seen before, a woman with a harsh face and cruel eyes, had come and told him his mother didn't want him.

Nobody wants you.

Nobody wants you.

Nobody wants you.

Sonny stared down the empty hallway—and felt something he hadn't felt in a long time. Loss.

* * *

The next day Sonny sent his luggage on ahead to the boat while he checked out of the hotel. When he stepped outside, a gust of damp sea air lifted his hair and crept down the collar of his jacket. His eyes turned to the sky above the wharf's end, searching for a glimmer of color—for Emily's kite. For the first time since coming to St. Genevieve he could detect no bright splash against the slate gray of the sky. He strained his eyes, but the kite wasn't there.

Doreen stopped beside him, her gaze following his, settling on the ferryboat that waited in the harbor. "Back to civilization," she said, satisfaction in her voice. "Back to cement sidewalks and neon lights. Traffic jams and cable TV."

Sonny was only half listening, his thoughts on Emily and the absent kite. He turned to Doreen. "Why don't you go on to the dock without me. I've got to check on something."

The satisfaction in Doreen's face was replaced by irritation. "The boat leaves in an hour. If you miss it, you'll be stuck here another week." She shuddered, from the chill or the thought of being stuck on the island, he didn't know. Maybe both.

"If I don't make it back in time, I'll hire a boat to take me to the mainland."

She grumbled and drew her head lower in her coat, like a turtle drawing into its shell.

Sonny didn't linger. Hunching his shoulders against the wind, he turned and headed for the narrow cobblestone street that led to the village kite-maker's shop.

He'd been by it more than a few times. It was a bright spot of color in an otherwise drab alley.

On the way, he passed a few people who looked as if they might be mainlanders getting an early start on the tourist season.

The narrow shop window was full of colorful kites. Fantasies and dreams. Emily's kites were like none he'd ever seen. He could imagine how they would capture the heart and imagination of a child.

There were unicorns and fairies, a huge butterfly, an unfamiliar winged creature—possibly a product of Emily's imagination. And there was a dragon, not as big as the one Emily had been flying the day she'd fallen into the ocean, but a dragon all the same, complete with bumpy tail and fiery eyes.

If I had a child, he thought, *I'd buy her one of Emily's kites.*

He turned the ornate gold knob and pushed a shoulder against the heavy wooden door. A bell jingled above his head as he stepped inside.

Once again he felt the strange sensation he'd felt upon entering Emily's house—the sensation of stepping into another world, maybe even another time. But here the feeling was enhanced and made a little mysterious by the heavy scent of fabric dye and damp, ancient wood.

It wasn't Emily who stepped from the small back room, but Claire.

She looked up at him, not with the hero worship this time, but worry. Her hands were twisting the hem of her shirt. "Emily's sick, so I'm watching the shop," she told him.

"Sick?"

"She's home in bed."

Claire chewed her bottom lip, as if wondering if she should say more. She stared up at him with her long-lashed green eyes. "Papa doesn't believe in doctors," she suddenly blurted out. "Not since Mama died. And anyway, there's no doctor on St. Genevieve."

Sonny's heart was thudding in his chest.

Claire's mouth began to tremble and her huge eyes suddenly filled with tears. "I'm worried. This morning, when I went in to see why Emily wasn't up yet, she didn't even know who I was."

Then, Claire began to cry.

"I-I tried to put out her kite like she always does, but the wind kept making it fold shut and I didn't want to lose it. Emily has always put out the kite. For years and years. And now I'm afraid if the kite's not out something bad might happen to Emily!"

Good Lord. Doreen had been right about these people and their superstitions!

Sonny wanted to run to Emily's house, but he couldn't leave the distraught Claire alone. He helped her lock up the shop, then she followed him to the harbor, where Doreen was waiting impatiently.

"Here—"

He shoved the folded kite into Doreen's hands. "Help Claire put this up."

"What is it?"

"A kite."

"Are you crazy?"

"Maybe. Probably. Look, I can't explain, but make them wait. Whatever happens, don't let the boat leave without me."

Then, leaving Claire with a bewildered Doreen, he hurried to Emily's house.

On the way there, he'd told himself that this was none of his business, that he had no claim on Emily Christian. But maybe he did. He'd pulled her from the ocean, hadn't he? Maybe that gave him some kind of right. He didn't know. He only knew that he'd spent his life on the outside looking in, and that now, for the first time since early childhood, he felt he had to step in and get involved.

His knock was answered by Tilly. Babbie poked her head out from behind her. It struck him that Tilly didn't look half as confident as she'd looked the other night. She seemed a little humble and subdued.

Worried. Like Claire.

"Emily's sick," she said. "And Daddy's gone to get her some cough medicine."

"I know Emily's sick. I came to see her."

Tilly seemed relieved to have an adult on whom to relinquish responsibility. "She's upstairs. Come on."

Emily's room was the first on the right at the top of the stairs. The shades were pulled, a lamp near the bed partially illuminated the sheet-draped figure on the bed.

It looked like a scene from a wake.

Fear reached out to him, but he pushed it away. In the glow of the lamp he could see the slight rise and fall of her chest beneath the white cotton gown. He let out a breath in relief.

He stepped into the room, moving to the bedside through warm, fever-laden air. Her cheeks were flushed bright red. A scruffy brown teddy bear, the fur rubbed completely away, was tucked neatly in beside her.

He felt his heart crack a little.

The scene saddened and frustrated him at the same time. It was like something a person might have witnessed a century ago.

He lay a hand against her brow. Her skin was hot and dry. Dehydration.

His touch caused her to stir.

Her eyelids fluttered open. Her beautiful eyes were glazed with fever and he wondered if she even saw him at all.

''Emily—'' Babbie whispered, coming up beside him, touching his hand as if for reassurance. ''Your prince came back.''

Emily struggled to focus her attention on the child. ''I see that, sweetheart,'' she said through dry, barely moving lips. Then her eyes drifted shut again.

''I gave her Bare Bear for company,'' Babbie whispered up at him.

''Emily's really sick, isn't she?'' asked Tilly.

''Yes,'' Sonny said. ''She needs a doctor.''

''Papa says doctors don't know what they're doing.''

''He says they're ducks,'' Babbie added.

''Quacks. He says they're quacks,'' Tilly said.

Sonny didn't want to scare them, but the ferry was leaving and he had to be sure Emily was on it. "All doctors aren't quacks," he said. "Emily is very sick. She needs a doctor now."

He tugged the sheets and blankets free of the mattress and began bundling them around Emily.

"What are you doing?" Tilly asked.

"Taking her to a doctor."

Tilly's grasp of the situation amazed him. She quickly dragged out a battered suitcase and started filling it with Emily's clothes.

Downstairs, a door slammed. A heavy footfall sounded on the stairs. "I got some cough syrup from the drugstore," came John Christian's voice drawing closer, along with his footsteps. "Clayton said—" He stopped just inside the room. "Mr. Maxwell... What?" He looked haggard, his eyes red-rimmed. Sonny watched as the man struggled to make sense of Sonny's presence in his sick daughter's room.

"Emily needs a doctor, not cough syrup," Sonny quickly explained. "My guess is that she has pneumonia. People die from pneumonia."

"Doctors!" John Christian raised a broad arm and gestured to something beyond the walls of the small bedroom. "I've got a wife lying in a grave on the hillside all because of doctors!"

"Senseless things happen. That's no reason to give up on the entire medical profession."

Sonny could see the indecision on John Christian's face, the glimmer of tears in the big man's eyes. And for the first time in his life, Sonny understood a little of the heavy burden of responsibility a parent must feel. The man's shoulders slumped. "My God," he said, more to himself than Sonny. "I don't know. My Emily. Sara's firstborn..."

Precious minutes were ticking away. Sonny prayed that Doreen could convince the ferryboat captain to delay departure.

"I know a doctor in New York," Sonny said. "He's a pulmonary specialist. One of the best in the country. He'll take good care of her."

John Christian closed his eyes, his face a mask of pain.

"There isn't much time," Sonny reminded him.

John Christian's eyes flew open and he looked at Sonny with anguish. "When a man meets the girl he wants to marry, he thinks his heart can be no fuller. But then he has children...."

He walked over to the bed and Sonny stepped back.

"It's hard to know what's best," John Christian said, looking down at Emily.

"She has no chance here," Sonny said quietly.

The man nodded in uneasy defeat, then bent and lifted his daughter from the bed as if she were a small child. "Come on, Emily lass. We're takin' you to a doctor."

On the way to the village Tilly and Babbie were left in the efficient hands of Annie McEntire.

In the harbor, the ferryboat was still waiting and Sonny silently thanked Doreen and her sometimes intimidating nature. As they stepped onto the gang-plank, he caught a glimpse of a purple unicorn fluttering against blue sky.

Chapter Five

Once Emily was at the hospital and on intravenous antibiotics, she began to improve almost immediately. By the third day she was well on her way to total recovery. She had even talked her father into returning to St. Genevieve by himself.

Now, on the fifth day, Sonny was sitting in Dr. Martin Berlin's office. Even though Martin had told him to quit hanging around the hospital disrupting things, Sonny hadn't listened. He couldn't seem to stay away. In fact, he'd just come from seeing Emily.

The doorknob turned and the office door flew open. "This is crazy!" Martin Berlin announced. Lab coat flapping about his knees, he slammed the door shut and strode across the small room to the window, tossing a stack of folders on his desk as he passed.

Sonny was used to Martin's theatrics. Martin sometimes participated in Little Theater productions, and some of the sweeping stage gestures and voice projection had carried over into his real life.

"The entire hospital is crawling with Sonny Maxwell groupies," Martin said, gesturing wildly.

Sonny locked his fingers over his stomach and stretched his legs out in front of him, crossing them at the ankles. "I've tried to keep a low profile."

Martin was on a roll. "And my nursing staff! They're walking around like a bunch of lovesick zombies. Just this morning, one of the nurses got the medicine orders mixed up. A patient almost ended up swallowing a suppository instead of a vitamin!"

Sonny had known Martin going on six years—ever since Sonny had donated enough money to add a children's research wing on to the hospital. Most doctors looked older than they really were. Martin was fifty, but looked forty. He was divorced, content, but one of the most highly strung characters Sonny had ever come across.

"What the hell do you do to them?" Martin asked. "There are at least thirty women out there right now, women just begging to be your love slave." He pointed toward the parking lot below. "From here, I can see a girl who can't be more than fifteen. She's holding up a sign that says, I want a piece of your action. Now what is a girl of fifteen doing with a sign like that?"

Sonny shrugged and laughed. "There's nothing I can do about it."

"It isn't funny. This is real life. Not one of your movies or ads. I'm scheduled for surgery this afternoon, and I don't know if there are any assistants left around here who don't have little hearts floating in front of their eyes. And that's not all. I can't leave this place without a dozen reporters shoving microphones in my face, demanding to know the scoop on you and Emily. I know you're trying to keep her name out of the tabloids, but I think you're going about it wrong. Why don't you just go out there and talk to them? If you don't tell them what's going on, they'll make something up."

"Since there's nothing tawdry to tell them, they'll make something up anyway."

"Well, this chaos can't go on any longer. This is a hospital, not your fan club headquarters."

"So what you're saying is you want me to leave and take Emily with me, right?"

"You make it sound as if I'm kicking her out." Martin came away from the window and perched himself on the edge of the desk, hands clasped in front of him, all doctor now. "Four or five days is the average stay for a pneumonia case. But Emily had some pretty badly damaged lung tissue. I'd like to keep her nearby for another week, then get a fresh set of X rays before she goes home. But with this mess outside, and my nurses..." He shook his head. "Something has to be done."

"Maybe she could stay in a hotel," Sonny suggested.

''You couldn't keep it a secret. The press would be hounding her within an hour. I have a better idea.'' Martin—normally an eye-to-eye man—rubbed the back of his neck and focused on something near the door. ''What about taking her to your place?''

''That won't work. My address is no secret—and then they *would* have something to talk about. I don't want Emily's name splashed all over the tabloids.''

''I'm not talking about your decoy apartment. I'm talking about your cabin.''

Sonny didn't take anybody to his cabin. Martin knew that. That's why he'd called his apartment a decoy. It was to satisfy all those people who thought they needed to know where he lived.

Sonny had deliberately bought his place in the woods because there was no other house in sight. Shortly after that, Martin began begging Sonny to let him fish in the stream near his cabin. Sonny had finally relented and Martin had liked the area so much he'd ended up buying the adjoining lot. Then he built a house on it. Now, on a clear night, when there weren't any leaves on the trees, Sonny could see the lights of Martin's property.

No, Martin couldn't be trusted.

And that wasn't the only thing that bugged Sonny about Martin. The man's specialty was cardiology and pulmonary care, but on the side he liked to dabble in psychology. Sometimes Sonny would catch him watching him, observing him as if he were some curious specimen. One time he'd even asked Sonny what he was afraid of.

"What do you say?" Martin asked. "Pretty decent idea, isn't it? Emily's off IVs. I could come and check on her every evening on my way home."

Sonny had always hated the thought of having his refuge invaded. He knew a time would come when the press would discover its whereabouts. When that happened, he didn't know where he'd go, didn't know where he'd run.

But for some reason the thought of Emily being at his place didn't seem so bad. And the more Sonny thought about it, the closer he came to actually *liking* the idea.

"I'm sure Emily won't mind," Martin said. "She's been stewing about the hospital bill. Yesterday, she asked me how much I made an hour."

"I hope you didn't tell her," Sonny said. "I'm taking care of the bill. I don't want her to even see it."

Martin's dark eyebrows lifted. "Oh yeah? Think again. You don't know her very well if you think Emily's the type to take a dime from anybody."

Martin was right. But it irritated Sonny to discover that Martin knew Emily so well.

Martin rubbed his hands together, then slapped his legs, a sure sign he was ready to wrap up the conversation. "So what do you think? Master plan, right?"

"How do we get her out of the hospital without being seen?"

"At night. By helicopter."

"Helicopter?"

Had Emily ever been in a helicopter? Sonny wondered. She might not go for it. He wouldn't want to force her into something she didn't want to do. After all, it was his fault the hospital was overrun with groupies, not hers.

"I don't know about the helicopter," Sonny said.

"With a helicopter there'd be no chance of your being tailed."

"I'll talk to Emily and let you know what we decide."

"There's no need." Martin smiled. "I'm heading that way right now."

Emily sat on the edge of the hospital bed. She was wearing the white sweatshirt and sweatpants Tilly had stuffed into her suitcase—bless her heart. Folded over one arm was the wool coat Doreen had loaned her when she'd dropped in for a visit. The rest of her things were packed. Dr. Berlin had been to see her, leaving medicine and a list of instructions.

Emily felt as if she had encroached upon Sonny's goodwill far too long already. But Dr. Berlin had explained that her presence in the hospital was creating chaos. She had suggested returning home, but the doctor refused to release her unless she remained nearby, under his care.

He'd told her that Sonny owned a secluded cabin, a hideaway. It would be an ideal place for her since it was near his own property.

She'd phoned her father, and he'd said it seemed the only solution, so she'd agreed to go. But that didn't mean she wasn't scared. She was. She was scared of going someplace strange, scared of going to that someplace with Sonny Maxwell, and scared of flying in a helicopter. Why, she'd never even been in an airplane.

At five minutes past midnight, Sonny stuck his head inside the door. "Your coach awaits."

The only concession he'd made to a disguise was a pair of sunglasses and an LA Laker's cap. He was dressed nondescript. If anything Sonny wore could be called nondescript. He was wearing a navy blue sweatshirt, stretched at the collar and hem, faded jeans and white jogging shoes.

While she'd never been one to ogle a man, Emily had to admit that Sonny made the most everyday clothes special, almost as if by lying next to his skin, they took on some of his persona. It was no wonder everyone wanted him to model their clothes. At that very moment, without even trying, he was cover material.

They moved quietly down the hallway, past the nurses' station to the elevators. After stepping inside, Sonny punched an unlabeled button, and the elevator took them to the roof of the six-floor building. Before stepping out, Sonny pushed Hold and helped Emily into her coat, making sure it was zipped up all the way. Then they stepped onto a lighted walkway that led to the landing pad and the waiting helicopter.

She and Sonny took the seat behind the pilot.

"Ever flown before?" Sonny asked.

She shook her head.

"Piece of cake. This helicopter is one of the best made," he said, helping her into her seat belt. "It works on the same lift principle as one of your kites."

She smiled, endeared by the fact that he was trying to calm her fears.

The pilot flicked a switch on the instrument panel and the blades began to rotate, picking up speed until Emily could no longer see them.

The craft seemed to bounce a little, then they were lifting away from the landing pad. The floor beneath Emily's feet shuddered. She squeezed her eyes shut and gripped Sonny's arm.

Of course it was ridiculous. If they crashed, he could do nothing, but she felt safer touching him, just knowing he was beside her.

When she finally got brave enough to open her eyes, the lights of the city were swirling away beneath them.

It was beautiful. Unreal.

Emily forgot her fear and leaned closer to the window.

As they went, Sonny pointed out various buildings until the lights became more scattered and they finally left the city behind.

A half hour later they were landing in the middle of an open area surrounded by trees. Sonny helped Emily from the helicopter, then grabbed her suitcase and guided her to the edge of the clearing.

"Close your eyes!" he shouted above the noise, pulling her head against his chest.

The helicopter lifted away, the giant blades whipping grass and leaves through the air.

Then they were enveloped in quiet and darkness. But Sonny's arm was around her and she felt safe.

He released his hold and flicked on a flashlight, directing the beam so it cut a path through the trees.

His warm fingers sought hers. "Come on."

She held on tightly as he led her through the dark woods.

In just a couple minutes they came to another cleared area. Nestled in the middle was a tiny A-frame house with gingerbread molding and shuttered windows. It looked like something from Hansel and Gretel.

"It's beautiful. I'd expected a cabin."

As if to explain why a man would have such a quaint house, Sonny shrugged and said, "It came with the property."

The inside turned out to be bigger than it appeared from the porch. But it was still small by most standards. The ground floor held a living room, a tiny kitchen and bathroom. One of the walls was covered with photographs.

Emily draped her coat over the couch and moved closer.

Most were black and whites, matted, but unframed. There were pictures of gnarled trees and vast skies. Pictures of old churches, old houses, broken-down fences.

"Did Doreen take these?" she asked, continuing to study the pictures before her. They were wonderful.

Sonny didn't answer.

She turned.

He'd tossed his cap and glasses on a nearby table. He was standing with his hands in the front pockets of his jeans, his expression a little uncomfortable, a little self-conscious maybe. She instantly understood. The pictures—they were his.

Her gaze was drawn back to the cluttered wall. Yes, she could see it now. She could see Sonny Maxwell there. The pictures had a remote, lonely quality.

"You took them, didn't you?"

"Yes."

The tone of his voice was strange...a little defensive. She could almost think he was a child being accused of some misdeed, or one who feared rejection.

"They're wonderful." What was she saying? They were better than wonderful. They were moving, touching. Painful. Beautiful. Like Sonny.

He seemed to relax. He moved nearer, his arm brushing her shoulder. "I took that one—" he pointed "—in Massachusetts. Near Old Salem."

It was a picture of a stone church. It had been shot from ground level, looking skyward, the steeple piercing a cloudless sky.

"Beautiful. So...moody..." *So sad.*

She wondered if he'd ever had a showing. Thinking of a showing turned her thoughts to Doreen. "Doreen must love your pictures."

"She's never seen them."

Why was he hiding these beautiful, haunting pictures? Pictures were to share, for other people to see.

"I can't believe you've never shown them to Doreen. She'd love them. They shouldn't be kept hidden here. Has anyone else seen them? Your family?"

A strange expression flitted across his features, then was gone. "No."

She suddenly realized that in the few times she'd been around him, he'd never spoken a word about his family. Or very much about himself, for that matter.

But tonight she'd discovered something. Sonny took beautiful, sad, haunting photographs that the world should see.

She studied the wall again, now realizing that in all the pictures, there wasn't a single photo of a person.

"No people?" she asked, hoping to sound offhand.

At first she thought he wasn't going to answer. Then he said, "I don't take pictures of people."

The strained remoteness was back in his voice.

Who are you, Sonny Maxwell? And what are you hiding behind those sad, secret eyes?

"This is one of my favorites," he said, obviously changing the subject.

The picture to which he pointed was a lighthouse.

"I love lighthouses," she told him.

This particular lighthouse had the caretaker's home attached—unlike the lighthouse on St. Genevieve where the light was separate from the house.

"My grandfather used to be the lighthouse keeper on St. Genevieve," she said. "I loved to climb the winding steps and watch him light the lamps."

"Is it still in operation?"

"No. About ten years ago they replaced it with an electronic buoy. It broke Grandpa's heart. He didn't live very long after that. Keeping the light had been everything to him."

She watched him as he thought over her words.

"That would be tough," he said, "to have such an important job replaced by a machine."

"He used to tell me the most wonderful stories about ships and men who had been saved by the light. Grandpa never took any credit himself. It was always the light."

"Who owns the lighthouse now?"

"The coast guard, but they're trying to sell it. I'm afraid if someone doesn't buy it soon, it might be torn down." She sighed, thinking about the plans she'd had. "I have to confess. It was my dream to be able to own the lighthouse myself someday."

"I hope you do."

She smiled a wistful smile. "Me too."

But she knew better. Because of her hospital stay, because of the bills she would have, her dream would never be more than that—a dream.

She reached up and straightened the picture. Before she could draw her hand away, his fingers wrapped around her wrist and gently brought it toward him. With a forefinger, he touched the purple-yellow bruise left by the IV needle.

"They had trouble finding my veins," she said, thinking how ugly her skin must look to someone as flawlessly perfect as Sonny.

Slowly, carefully, tenderly, he lifted her hand and pressed his lips to the bruise. With her hand still near his mouth, close enough so she could feel the stir of his breath, he looked into her eyes and said, "That's because mermaids don't have veins."

She laughed a little, but inside her heart was hammering madly. Here she was in the middle of nowhere, with a man she hardly knew. A man who was kissing her hand and staring at her with soft, heavy-lidded eyes. A man who had been labeled the sexiest man in the world, a man all women craved.

Almost as if he read her mind, he said, "I'd never hurt you, Emily."

Her alarm subsided. Or had it been alarm at all? Maybe it was excitement that made her heart race and her breath catch.

"I'd never hurt you," he repeated. "You know that, don't you?"

"Yes."

"Good."

He let go of her hand. "You better get to bed. Dr. Berlin's orders."

She'd been tired earlier, but now, *now* she was wide awake. Emily, who had never told as much as a white lie in her life, said, "I am a little tired."

"The bedroom's upstairs." He lifted her suitcase.

She thought about all the women he must know, all the women who had shared his bed. But not her. She hadn't been brought up that way.

"Where will you sleep?" she asked.

His eyes went to the couch.

"I didn't know I'd be taking your bed. I'll sleep on the couch."

"It's okay. I can sleep anyplace." He smiled, his eyes asking her to let it be okay.

What could she do but smile back?

Two days later Martin stopped by to check on his patient.

Emily was sitting on the edge of the bed, Martin beside her while Sonny hovered anxiously in the bedroom doorway. He didn't like the idea of Martin unbuttoning Emily's shirt, touching Emily's soft skin.

Martin looked over his shoulder. "Would you give us some privacy?" he asked, his hand poised at the buttons of Emily's shirt.

When Emily had been discharged from the hospital Martin had taken Sonny aside and told him that there were no restrictions, that she could do whatever she wanted as long as it didn't entail strenuous, heavy breathing. With that, he'd winked and Sonny had ground his teeth.

Now, thinking about that episode and Martin's lecherous wink, Sonny was loath to leave the room. He should have taken Emily to somebody else, he thought, but knew he didn't mean it. Martin was the best. And Martin would never do anything unethical. It was just that . . . *damn*, Sonny didn't like him being so familiar with Emily. It scared her. Sonny could tell.

"Do you mind?" Martin repeated.

Emily and Martin were both watching him, Martin with a little bit of a smirk. Sonny could see that Martin knew he didn't like him touching Emily. It was clear he found it amusing. Martin had a strange sense of humor. On the other hand, Emily's expression was pleading and embarrassed. With her eyes, she was begging him to leave. Sonny realized he was making an uncomfortable situation even more uncomfortable.

He was poised to back away when Martin said, "Why not go chop some wood?" Humor still danced in his eyes.

He'd obviously seen the woodpile. Whenever Sonny's thoughts focused on Emily, whenever he found himself dwelling upon the softness of her skin, the blueness of her eyes, about how warm and sexy she looked in his bed, about how her gown would creep up around her thighs while she slept...about how badly he wanted to make love to her in that bed, or on the soft clover near the brook...or under the pine trees...under the moonlit sky... Whenever he caught himself thinking of any of those things, he went outside and chopped wood.

So far, he had chopped enough wood to last him several winters.

Arms crossed at his chest, Sonny pushed himself away from the wall. "I won't be far," he muttered, silently cursing Martin and his x-ray vision.

Emily heard the front door close.

Instead of putting the stethoscope to her chest, Martin got up, strode to the window and looked out. "There he goes. Straight for the woodpile." He turned back to Emily. "How are you two getting along?"

Her hand hovered near the buttons of her blouse. How does someone get along with Sonny, she wondered. "He's a very private person," she said.

"No kidding. I first met him six years ago, when he donated money to add a children's wing to the hospital. I consider him a friend, but I really don't know him any better today than I did when we first met. But you've done something to break through that shell of his."

She shook her head. "I'm sure I don't know him nearly as well as you do."

Martin shook his head. "You've gotten to him somehow. This place is sacred. It's his sanctuary. Nobody, I mean *nobody* comes here. Before you arrived on the scene, I'd never gotten past the porch. And now I'm only here because you're here."

He sat down next to her on the edge of the bed, adjusting his stethoscope. She was hardly aware of the examination, caught up as she was in what he'd just told her about being allowed here—Sonny's secret place.

"Sounds good," Martin said, removing the stethoscope. "I'll talk to Sonny about bringing you to the hospital the day after tomorrow. We'll take some X rays and if they look okay, we'll send you home. How does that sound?"

Suddenly she wasn't sure how it sounded. It would mean saying goodbye to Sonny.

* * *

The next day Sonny felt kind of silly, like someone reciting lines from a corny movie, but he asked Emily if she'd like to go for a walk.

She smiled up at him and his heart thudded in his chest. "I'd love to."

He'd never wanted anybody to see his place. Now, suddenly, he couldn't wait for Emily to see his favorite spots.

They walked around the spring-fed pond where he sometimes fished. Spring was Sonny's favorite time of year. Maybe because everything was new. The grass was at its greenest, the air its cleanest. But he didn't share those thoughts with Emily. He could only give away so much.

"There are a hundred acres here," he told her as they walked over the new grass. He wasn't trying to impress her with the amount of land he owned—one hundred acres wouldn't begin to keep a farmer in business. He simply used it to gauge the distance and space between himself and the rest of the world.

Emily laughed and asked if he was like Owl in *Winnie the Pooh*.

He didn't get it.

She must have noticed his puzzlement, because she said, "Owl lived in the hundred-acre wood, remember?"

"Sure." But he didn't remember. He'd never read any kid's stories. Whenever people made reference to a storybook character, he felt like a visitor from another planet.

He took her to his favorite place: Spring Hollow. It couldn't even be seen until you were right on it—a huge opening in the ground filled with moss-covered boulders bigger than houses. Water poured from the side of one rocky crevice, cascading over delicate ferns and moss.

"It's beautiful," Emily said, her voice full of awe.

She meant it. He could tell. And he was glad that she liked it here. This was new to him, sharing the beauty of nature with someone. He felt a brief moment of panic, afraid for himself.

"I can feel the coolness from here," she said, stepping closer to the side.

Sonny grabbed her arm, afraid for her.

"The hollow creates a cave affect," he explained, gently urging her back. "It's cool in the winter, warm in the summer. The Indians used to store food in some of those small caves."

He would have liked to have taken her down to the bottom, where the waterfall tumbled into a crystal-clear pool. But the stone sides were almost straight up and down. And they were damp, slippery. It was a strenuous climb for someone who hadn't been sick. Maybe another time.

Again he felt that strange disquiet as he remembered there would be no other time.

On the way back to the cabin, Sonny stopped to point out some plants that Emily may not have seen living on St. Genevieve—plants that required shade and the protection of trees and mulch to survive harsh winters. He showed her a jack-in-the-pulpit and ginseng weed. He pulled a leaf from a nearby tree and handed it to her. "Some people say if you carry a hickory leaf in your pocket, it will bring good luck."

"I think I've had my share of good luck already," she said as she took the leaf.

It was getting late. The air was cooling. Emily should be inside.

Sonny knew what he was doing: trying to prolong the day, trying to save it.

"I have to go in to the city tomorrow," he said. "I have a meeting with Doreen."

"Don't worry about me. Don't give me a second thought."

But he would. A second and a third. He'd wanted her to look a little sad that he had to leave on what would probably be their last day together. But she was smiling, her eyes wide and honest, her face like an angel's. "I'm glad I got a chance to see your place. Now, instead of thinking of you in the noise and confusion of New York City, I'll remember you here—where it's green and peaceful."

He didn't know why she would say such a thing, why it would matter where she remembered him. But he was glad that it mattered.

Side by side, they walked back to the cabin.

Chapter Six

Sonny poured himself a cup of coffee and instantly regretted it. It wasn't as if he didn't know any better. He did. Doreen was famous for her awful coffee. He took a suspicious sip. An acid-hickory taste filled his mouth. He shuddered. "You trying to see if this will ferment?"

"Things get better with age," Doreen said, leaning back in her chair, New York City skyscrapers framed in the window behind her. "Isn't that what you're always telling me?"

He dumped the coffee back into the pot, shut off the warmer, then went to the adjoining bathroom and poured the entire contents down the drain, hoping it wouldn't eat up the pipes.

"Speaking of age," Doreen said as he came out of

the bathroom, "I went to see Martin Berlin yesterday."

Sonny picked up an open bag of pretzels. "Oh yeah?" He hadn't expected her to keep the appointment. She never had time for anything but her work. Sonny plopped down in the white vinyl couch, practically sinking to the floor. Cellophane crinkled as he pulled a pretzel from the bag.

"That friend of yours had his hands all over me."

"Martin?" His head came up.

"Yes, Martin. *Doctor* Martin Berlin." Doreen fumbled around, rearranging pencils in the pencil holder. "He made me take off my blouse. I'm too old to be taking off my blouse in front of a stranger."

"Doreen, he's a heart and lung specialist," he said around a pretzel. "He's supposed to see you without a shirt. He's supposed to have his hands all over you— you know that." He held the open bag of pretzels out to her, but she shook her head.

"If you'd never seen me before," she said, "how old would you say I was?"

So that's what this was all about. Her age. He looked at her. Really looked at her. And he had to admit that she'd aged a lot in the last few years. Her hair was more gray than black, her face more fine-lined. It filled him with a vague feeling of alarm.

"You'd think old, wouldn't you? Admit it."

Sonny hedged. "What does age have to do with Martin Berlin?" Another thought hit him. He dropped the bag of pretzels and leaned forward. "Is something wrong? You're not sick, are you?"

"He said I'm healthy except for being a little run-down. Nothing that some iron tablets won't cure."

"Then . . . ?"

She picked up a pencil, turned it sideways and closely examined the engraving. "He asked me out."

Martin and Doreen? Sonny's initial reaction was shock—they seemed totally incompatible. But the more he thought about it . . . They were both stubborn, both hard to get along with at times. They might deserve one another. "Look at it this way," he said, "if you went out with him, he wouldn't be a stranger anymore."

"I'm not going."

"Why not?"

"Why not? I'm too old, that's why not."

"There's only what—seven years difference in your ages."

"That's not what I mean. I mean I'm too set in my ways." She jammed the pencil into the holder. "And he saw me with my blouse off," she added, more to herself than to Sonny.

"Good Lord, Doreen. I never had you figured for a prude. In fact—" he smiled "—I seem to recall a party where you went swimming in your skivvies."

Doreen blushed. Actually blushed.

Well, well.

"That was a long time ago," she said. "I'm too old for that dating nonsense. I wouldn't know how to act. Should I let him open the door? Let him pull out my chair? Give me a good-night kiss? Should I invite him up for a drink? When a man asks a woman out, he always expects something in return. A meal in exchange for a roll in the hay.''

"Martin wouldn't be like that. You're making generalizations.''

"Because that's what *generally* happens. No, too many complications. I don't need complications.'' She waved a hand in the air, then began shuffling the papers on her desk, searching for her glasses. "Forget about Martin. Let's just get down to business.''

"Fine.'' She was really worked up so Sonny let it drop.

"Carol liked the shots we took on St. Genevieve. They'll use them in the fall issue, but along with the photos, they want to run a story on you.''

"No way.''

"Why not?''

"You know why not. I don't do interviews. They add stuff, twist words around, screw up everything you say. If I say, I hate to see animals suffer, they print, Sonny hates animals. You can't win.''

"What if we got final approval? It would be a chance to tell it like it is.''

"No.''

"You know what I think? I think you're afraid to let anybody see the real Sonny Maxwell.''

"The *real* Sonny Maxwell? What's that supposed to mean?''

"It means you hide behind that gorgeous face and great body. That's what it means.''

He snorted. "You and Martin *would* make a great pair. You could sit around and psychoanalyze one another."

"Don't make me laugh."

"You're way off base if you think I'm going to jump on the childhood repression bandwagon. I never had my favorite stuffed animal taken from me. I was never served rats for lunch. Nobody ever laid a hand on me. What are you looking at me like that for? Interviews are an invasion of privacy, and that's all there is to it."

"No more of an intrusion than the article *Celebrity World* ran on you."

"Was that the one where I used astral projection to enter a woman's hotel room and make love to her?"

"Same rag, different story. You mean you haven't seen it? Oh, that's right. You've been doing your Walden Pond thing." She rummaged through some more stuff on her desk, pulled out a limp, cheap-looking magazine and tossed it at him.

He caught the tabloid and unfolded it. The sensationalized headline jumped out at him. Heartthrob Sonny Maxwell Shacks Up With Fisherman's Daughter.

Sonny went very still, all of his attention focused on the paper in his hands. There was a grainy picture below the headline—a close-up of Emily, obviously taken with a telephoto lens.

He dug through the rest of the paper until he came to the article. It had merited center spread, complete with more grainy, out-of-focus photos.

Pictures taken at his cabin. So, they'd finally found it. Surprisingly it wasn't the fact that they'd discovered his cabin that angered him. It was what they'd done to Emily.

There was a photo of her standing on the porch, staring into the distance, in the direction of home. It hadn't occurred to him that she might be homesick. That realization brought a lightning jab of unease, once again reminding him that she would be leaving soon.

There was another picture. This one was of both of them strolling through the woods—taken only yesterday. Their heads were bent together, like two lovers. He'd been showing her something, maybe the hickory leaf. At the time, he'd thought they'd been alone.

His knuckles were white from gripping the paper so tightly. He didn't realize his jaw was clenched until it began to ache.

"At least they didn't say you were both beamed aboard an alien vessel," Doreen said.

He threw the paper down, disgust and anger raging through him.

"These rags are always picking on you," Doreen said, obviously surprised at the severity of his reaction. "It's never bothered you before. What's the big deal?"

He paced to the window and leaned both hands against the sill. A jet was reflected in the smoky glass of the adjacent high-rise. "This is different. This involves Emily."

Emily.

Tomorrow she would be going back to St. Genevieve. On St. Genevieve they had a drugstore that carried *Celebrity World*.

He could visualize somebody on the island casually picking up the magazine. Then they would say, hey, look here. People would gather round. Then someone would read parts of it out loud and everybody would laugh. He imagined Emily stepping inside the store and everyone falling silent. She would wonder why they were all staring. Someone would snicker, then her gaze would drop to the tabloid in their hands.

He squeezed his eyes shut, as if by doing so he could block out the image.

I'm sorry, Emily. God, I'm sorry.

He'd never meant to hurt her, never meant to drag her down with him.

People could be so cruel. Nobody knew that better than Sonny. And Emily was so open, so guileless. Up until now—until she'd met him—she'd had no reason to be otherwise.

Emily.

His next thought hit him like a jolt: She was alone at the cabin. That meant the lowlife who'd taken the pictures might be there right now.

Not wasting any more time, he turned and lunged for the door. "I've got to go," he shouted over his shoulder.

And he left, slamming the door behind him.

As the rattling photos on the wall settled back into place, Doreen smiled to herself. In all the years she'd known Sonny, she'd never seen him slam a door. This was interesting. Perhaps the real Sonny Maxwell, the one who had disappeared as a child, was about to be reborn.

All-terrain tires hummed over asphalt. The battered canvas top flapped in the wind. With the accelerator pressed to the floorboard, Sonny's battered Jeep topped out at sixty miles per hour, an inconvenience Sonny normally didn't mind. This was the first time he wished it would go faster.

Hands gripping the steering wheel, he drove. And as he drove, his anger increased with each rotation of the tires.

He was used to the lies, used to the public floggings, the witch trials. For him, that kind of thing just went with the territory. But Emily didn't deserve to be degraded like that.

His jaw hurt; his teeth were clenched again. He consciously made an effort to stop, only to have his jaw start aching a few minutes later.

He approached the turn, slowed, then pulled off the highway to follow a gravel road. At the almost inaccessible lane that led to his property, he spotted a blue Chevy Impala parked half in the ditch. Cursing, Sonny put the Jeep into four-wheel-drive and headed up the rocky incline.

His place was inaccessible, but not inaccessible enough. He hadn't wanted to put up security fences. There were too many fences in the world.

Branches scraped the windows. He passed No Trespassing signs and No Hunting signs—small pieces of tin and painted words that apparently meant nothing. It seemed that some people could only understand fences.

Then up ahead he could see glimpses of his cabin—flashes of redwood through green leaves.

Finally he was close enough to see Emily standing on the porch. Someone was with her.

He tromped down on the clutch and put the Jeep in neutral, road dust drifting in the windows and cracks as he slowed. Before the Jeep had rolled to a complete stop, Sonny shouldered the door open. Then, with tunnel vision, he ran toward the house, toward the porch, toward the blond curly-haired man with the tablet and pencil.

The two on the porch watched his approach—Emily, with puzzlement, the reporter with dawning dismay.

It was as if all the anger he'd never used in his life surfaced now, in defense of Emily. Sonny charged up the steps.

The man raised a bent arm in a protective gesture and took a step back.

Sonny grabbed two handfuls of khaki vest—a vest that read Charlie Painter on the pocket—and shoved the man up against the wall, his tablet and pencil skittering across the enamel floor.

"Sonny!"

The shock in Emily's voice brought a flash of shame to Sonny, but the shame couldn't come close to outweighing the anger that was pouring through him.

"Sonny! Stop! Don't hit him!"

"This is private property," he told the man, punctuating each word by giving the guy's shoulders an extra shove against the wall. "Do you know what that means?"

"Sonny—he was just asking me some questions."

She didn't understand. "He's been telling lies about you," Sonny said over his shoulder, not taking his eyes from the reporter.

The reporter wasn't some punk, as he'd looked from a distance. Up close, his face was old, a map of fine wrinkles; eyes yellow from a lifetime spent in smoky rooms, bloodshot from too much booze. One of those guys who'd had it rough from day one.

Sonny tried to squelch the surge of sympathy he was feeling, but couldn't quite manage it. The guy was just so damn pathetic. He couldn't hit him. "Do you know what can happen if you don't obey the private property signs?" he asked. "You can be shot."

"Hey—" The reporter put up both hands, palms out. "I was just doing my job, that's all. Just doing my job."

"Is part of your job telling lies?"

"Sonny—" Emily said from just behind his shoulder. "Let him go—please."

There was no way he could ignore her soft plea. He let go. But before stepping back he checked the multitude of pockets on the man's vest and pulled out two rolls of film. He tossed them over one shoulder, then grabbed the reporter's camera. He opened it, removed the film, then snapped the camera shut and shoved it at the man's stomach. "Now get the hell out of here."

The reporter didn't hesitate. He took off up the lane, but before disappearing behind the grove of trees he stopped and shouted, "You'll be sorry!"

Sonny wasn't worried. He'd heard the threat a million times.

Then the man made an obscene gesture with one hand—and Sonny wished he'd hit him.

For the last three hours—ever since reading the headlines in Doreen's office, Sonny had been running on adrenaline fueled by anger. Now the anger faded, leaving him feeling empty, hollow.

He sank to the steps, elbows on his knees. It hadn't done any good to rough up the reporter. The words and pictures had already been printed, the damage already done.

Now he had to tell Emily.

Quietly she sat down beside him on the steps. Her small, unconscious gesture of friendship was bittersweet. In a few moments he would have to tell her about the article in the paper, and she would wish she hadn't sat beside him, wish she hadn't had anything to do with him at all.

How could he tell her?

The rolls of film were lying in the grass near the bottom step. He picked them up and pulled out the film, exposing it to the light. When he was done, he dropped them on the ground, brown spiral curls of hurt and defamation.

"Did you ever think about how different the world would be if we had no way of recording images?" he asked. It was a subject he often pondered. "People wouldn't be able to obsess about celebrities."

"Yes, but what about the photos you take?"

"They aren't real. They're done with light and shadow, angles, distortion of depth of field. It's all an illusion, all make-believe."

But Emily, he thought. *She* was real. Funny how the first time he'd seen her he'd thought she had seemed of another time and place, another world. Now she was the most real person Sonny had ever known. Maybe it was because her soul was still intact. It hadn't been stolen.

Until now, a voice in his head corrected. Until the reporter had taken a picture of her, exposing and giving her soul to the world.

He sighed and looked out toward the grove of trees. Was there someone out there right now, watching them? Yesterday, the grove had been a protection, a fortress against the world. Now it was a cover for prying eyes.

As he stared at nothing, wondering what words to say, he felt her small hand lightly touch his shoulder. "I'm sorry, Sonny. I'm sorry they found your special place."

Her voice was thick, as if she were fighting back tears. Her hand was a comfort he had no right to take. Her reputation was ruined, and she was worried about him.

"You won't get rid of the cabin, will you?"

"No. I could never do that."

How was he going to tell her about the article?

He didn't. He ended up going to the Jeep and getting the paper. Without a word, he handed it to her. Then he made himself watch as she read it. Some people would have skimmed it, but Emily took her time, reading the article from beginning to end. And when her cheeks flushed pink, he knew she was reading the part about their being lovers.

When she had finished, she closed the paper and sat there, hands clasped neatly at her knees, her eyes staring blankly ahead.

He wondered if it was the first time she'd ever been hurt like this. The first time was the worst.

She made a little sound in her throat. "I'm not like that," she said. "I'm not using you. I'm not after your money." She blushed. "I'm not after your body."

"I know." He couldn't help the twinge of regret he felt. After all, he was flesh and blood and hormones.

"When I was little, there were a couple of boys who made fun of me because of my light hair," she said. "At that time, it was almost white. They called me names." She gave a little self-conscious laugh. "Nothing very imaginative, but it hurt all the same."

Sonny wished he'd been there. He would have made them take it back.

"I ran home crying. It wasn't so much what they said, but why. I couldn't understand why they would want to be cruel simply for the sake of being cruel. I still don't understand. Why do people print lies?"

"Because people want to read lies. Lies sell papers."

"He didn't seem like a bad man. I've always thought the most important thing a person could do as they live their life, is be kind to others. I used to think everybody thought that way."

She looked at him, her eyes full of confusion and hurt, begging him to make sense of something that made no sense.

He wished to God he could take the hurt from her eyes, shelter her from the world. A person had to be on guard, careful. But he didn't want to tell her that. He didn't want her to change. "Some people take advantage of kindness," he said.

She picked up the notebook that had fallen to the porch floor. He watched as she read the reporter's notes, her eyes moving back and forth. When she was done, she shut the notebook. Without looking at him, she got to her feet and went inside.

Sonny picked up the notebook and opened it.

It's easy to see why Sonny Maxwell chose Emily Christian as his lover. She has an open, earthy quality that spells sexy. Like Lil' Abner's Daisy. Big bedroom eyes that say she's hot, ready and willing to please her man.

He should have hit him. No, he should have killed him.

Sonny sat on the porch for a long time. After the sun was gone, he went inside and burned the notebook in the fireplace. While he watched the edges of paper curl, he came to a decision.

He found Emily upstairs, packing. He didn't go any closer than the doorway. He wrapped his fingers around the wooden doorjamb and hung on. "I'm sorry, Emily."

She looked up from the suitcase and smiled. Her eyes were red-rimmed. She'd been crying.

Mermaid tears.

Something twisted inside him.

But it was her smile that hurt the most. It was sad and wistful **and** brave, defying the moisture in her eyes. A brave front. She was learning. She'd grown her first layer of defense against the world.

"It's okay, Sonny."

"I have an idea."

She shook her head. "There's nothing that can be done. I'd rather not talk about it."

"There's something we could do to stop the gossip."

She looked up, a puzzled frown on her innocent face. Suddenly he was scared. More scared than he'd been when he'd handed her the article.

He didn't want to let her go. Now that he'd found her, he didn't want to lose her.

He swallowed and said, hoping to sound offhand, "We could get married."

Her big blue eyes grew even larger. She started to say something, stopped, then started again. "Married?" She tested the word in her mouth as if she'd never said it before.

"This is all my fault," he said.

Don't blow it. Don't let her see how much you want her.

"Getting married would stop the lies. And it would get the press off my back. They don't seem to be interested in staid, married men."

When she still didn't answer, he rushed on. "It could be temporary. Just for show."

"You mean . . . kind of like a pretend marriage?"

"Yeah, pretend."

She moved her hands in nervous confusion. Her eyes looked at everything but him. "Getting married would only give credence to the lie." Now she looked at him. "Thank you, but no. I couldn't possibly marry you."

Her rejection was like a physical blow. Mentally, he staggered back. Once again, he was a child being shoved away.

She doesn't want you. Nobody wants you.

It was hard to breathe. But he had to say something, had to let her know that her rejection didn't matter.

He called upon his acting talent, but then he'd never been much of an actor. What had one critic said?

Sonny Maxwell was a pretty package with nothing inside.

"Yeah, well." He managed a shrug. "It was just an idea."

Blindly, he turned and left.

Emily stood staring at the empty doorway.

Sonny was gone, but the small room still reverberated with dark, powerful emotions. There hadn't been any visual colors, but she had felt a black despair of the most staggering magnitude. And it was still here, pressing down upon her.

He'd wanted her to say yes.

She couldn't believe it.

Yes.

When she hadn't, his face had gone still. Pain and despair had filled the room.

She slowly closed her suitcase. Then she went downstairs.

Sonny was sitting on the couch, staring at a small pile of ashes in the fireplace. His sunstreaked, wind-tousled hair lay shaggily over the collar of his shirt. One fine-boned hand rested on a bent knee.

Love for him rushed over her and through her, scaring her, overwhelming her. She was in love with someone she barely knew.

She was in love with Sonny Maxwell.

Softly, she spoke his name. He turned and looked at her. The pain wasn't apparent now. He'd gotten it under control. He waited, watching quietly.

"I'll marry you," she whispered.

A spark leapt into his eyes, a flash of joy, of life, then it was gone, covered up. But it had been enough to warm her.

He got to his feet and came to stand in front of her. He took both of her hands in his.

It seemed most unlikely, but she had the strangest feeling that he was too overcome to speak.

Nonsense.

He pulled her close, pressing a soft, deliberate kiss on her lips. Then he was enfolding her in his arms, pulling her to him, holding her tightly, his fingertips in her hair, against her scalp, pressing her ear to his heart.

"Are you sure, Emily?"

"Yes. I'm sure." So very sure.

Chapter Seven

For Emily, saying yes had come naturally. She loved Sonny. And even though she knew he didn't love her, she sensed that he needed her, and she harbored a secret hope that in time that need would turn to love.

In the fairy tales Babbie was so fond of, the stories always ended when the princess said yes. Emily hadn't looked ahead to the reality of getting married. There was a marriage license to buy, blood tests to take, decisions to make. It was overwhelming.

She was thankful Sonny was so organized, so practical.

"Have you thought about where you want to live?" he asked as they stood in the courthouse waiting to apply for their marriage license.

Reality. "I don't know." In truth, she hadn't thought beyond the present. But she didn't think

Sonny would be able to stand the isolation of St. Genevieve, and now she had to face the possibility of a life away from her family, away from her little island.

When they finished with the marriage application, he grasped her by the elbow. "We have another matter to take care of before we leave."

"Another matter?"

"Come on—"

His eyes were shining with some strange inner excitement, some secret. She'd never seen him look so alive.

They took the elevator to the third floor and a cramped office where they met a man who looked as if he might be a lawyer.

"Everything has been taken care of," the man said. He handed Sonny an official-looking document. "We just need Emily's signature on the bottom line."

Sonny passed the paper to Emily.

A deed. A deed to the St. Genevieve lighthouse.

She looked up at Sonny, unable to take it all in. "I—I don't understand...."

"It's a present. A wedding present."

Her grandfather's lighthouse?

Half-formed thoughts collided in her mind. *The lighthouse.* It was so sudden, such a surprise, more than she could grasp. Here he was, giving her something she had thought unattainable, something beyond her reach. And since the lighthouse included the attached cottage, it might also mean that they would live on St. Genevieve.

She glanced up at Sonny, then back at the paper in her hands. He was already under the impression that she was using him to save her name. What would he think if she accepted such a gift—one he knew she wanted so desperately? To him, it might seem that she was using him again, this time in order to own the lighthouse.

Sonny was more important than the lighthouse. Much more.

He looked so pleased with himself. She hated to disappoint him, but she knew she must. She handed the paper back to him. "I can't accept this, Sonny. It's too much."

"I went to a lot of work to get this arranged. You have to accept it." He stuck the paper back in her hand and led her to a nearby table. He picked up a pen and worked it between her fingers. "Sign the paper, Emily. The lighthouse should be yours."

"Sonny, I can't possibly accept such a gift."

"Don't think of it as a gift. Think of it as saving a piece of history. If you don't take it, it might be torn down."

"Come on, Emily. Sign it." He stepped back, crossed his arms over his chest, and gave her a smile that made her melt inside. "Sign it for me."

And so she signed it for Sonny, and became the new owner of the St. Genevieve lighthouse.

Sonny and Emily were married in the little white church on St. Genevieve Island—the church where Sara and John Christian had been married and where

Emily had been baptized. The church where Emily still sang in the Sunday choir.

Emily had told Sonny that a courthouse wedding would have been fine, but he had somehow seen through her brave smile and insisted the wedding take place on St. Genevieve, with her family present.

Now, dressed in Sara Christian's wedding gown, Emily stood by Sonny's side before Pastor John.

With this ring... I thee wed...

Dressed in black tails, Sonny bowed his head toward her, a shaft of sunlight striking his hair, reflecting off the golden streaks. If ever a man could be called beautiful, Emily thought, it was Sonny Maxwell.

She lifted her hand to accept the ring. Feeling disembodied, she watched her hand tremble, helpless to stop the tremors. Then she felt the steadiness of Sonny's sure grip as he slid the plain gold band on her finger.

With this ring, I thee wed... forsaking all others... 'til death do us part....

Then it was Emily's turn. She repeated the vows, her voice shaking as badly as her hands. Sonny had to help guide the gold band on his own finger. Then he squeezed her hand and gave her a reassuring smile. "This will all be over in a few more minutes," he whispered.

No, it was just beginning. It wasn't until now that the full significance of what she was doing hit her. She'd made a promise before God.

When the vows were completed, Pastor John said, "You may kiss the bride."

Through a blur of confused and churning emotions, Emily saw Sonny smile down at her. Then he bent and brushed his lips lightly across hers.

Like a promise. A sweet, sweet promise.

Her eyes were about to drift closed when his lips left hers. Pastor John indicated that they should face the congregation.

They turned.

The pews were full. All of St. Genevieve had turned out to see Sonny Maxwell make an honest woman of Emily Christian.

"May I introduce Mr. and Mrs. Sonny Maxwell."

The sound of applause echoed through the church.

Emily was hardly aware of being escorted back down the aisle and out the double doors. Sunshine touched her face and a crisp wind tugged at her skirt, molding it to her legs.

And then people were there, pumping hands, kissing cheeks. Emily was enveloped in frail arms, pressed into matronly bosoms; Kelly McFarlin gave her a broad wink. Her father, with a hint of suspicious moisture in his dark eyes, hugged her to him, then pounded his new son-in-law on the back.

Emily's sisters were making their presence known. Babbie couldn't seem to hold still. She was dancing an excited circle around everybody. For her, they were living the perfect happy ending. Claire was in her glory, vacillating between holding her head extremely high and watching Sonny with dreamy eyes. Tilly was trying to maintain a bored facade, but when it came time to throw the rice, she dropped all pretense of disinterest. In fact, she became so caught up in the festivities that John Christian was forced to halt her pitching arm in mid-throw, firmly reminding her to *gently* toss the rice.

Doreen was busy snapping pictures, documenting the occasion. Martin Berlin, looking dashing in a tux, hovered near her shoulder. Occasionally Doreen would flash him a studied look of irritation. Then he would lean close and whisper something in her ear and Doreen would reward him with a reluctant smile.

Sonny broke away from the cluster of chatting people and strode toward his Jeep, which he'd had ferried to the island. It was old and, as Sonny had put it, didn't have much go. Emily liked the fact that Sonny wasn't obsessed with speed. Another stereotype shattered.

She was still staring in the direction Sonny had gone when Doreen came up and surprised her by giving her a quick hug. And Emily could have sworn she detected a glimmer of tears in the woman's eyes. With his dry surgeon's palm, Martin shook her hand.

Sonny pulled up in the Jeep. He set the emergency brake, then came around to her side.

"Sorry about the wheels. A Jeep and a wedding gown don't quite go together."

Emily thought it charming. "It's wonderful," she assured him.

He helped her up, tucking her skirt inside before shutting the door. Then he slid behind the steering wheel.

They pulled away, Emily waving goodbye. Claire, Babbie and Tilly stood beside their father, waving as if Emily were boarding a ship to journey far, far away.

And in a way, she was.

The Jeep rattled over the rutted lane. In the short time Emily had been gone, the grass had turned a vivid green, and the huge baseball-size dandelions St. Genevieve was famous for had opened. They covered the gently sloping hills like fields of bright yellow carpet.

The St. Genevieve lighthouse stood on an outcropping on the north end of the island. It was attached to the quaint cottage by a wooden rampway.

Sonny stopped in front of the white picket fence, shut off the engine, then came around to help Emily out.

They went through the arched gateway and up the cobblestone walk. Their hard-soled dress shoes echoed sharply against the porch floor.

"I made a couple phone calls and found someone to clean up the place." Sonny swung open the wooden door and stood aside.

It had been four years since Emily had been here. She was surprised and delighted to find that it hadn't changed very much. The wooden church pew, worn smooth and shiny from all those devoted churchgoers, still stood near the door, next to the oak hat rack.

It was a strange feeling—very much like coming home. She felt that if she listened very closely she might be able to hear her own childish voice echoing across the gleaming paste-waxed floors. She could almost see her grandfather reach in his pocket to pull out his watch, then look out the west window, toward the setting sun.

"'Bout time to light the lamps, Emmie girl," he would say. Then he'd take her small hand and together they'd head up the planked walkway that led to the lighthouse.

The leather-bound log book still lay on the tiny walnut stand next to the pew—just as it always had. Emily traced a finger across the faded gold letters. KEEPERS OF THE FLAME. She picked up the book. Then carefully, so as not to crack the glue on the spine, she opened it.

Inside were the names of all the caretakers. The first entry dated back to the year 1785, and the last was Emily's grandfather, Nathaniel Christian.

Along with the names, there were dates and accounts of shipwrecks, replacement of reflective lenses, the amount of oil used in a year, and the date they changed from lard oil to mineral oil.

Sonny was reading over her shoulder. She could feel his warmth against her back. "The lighthouse was never converted to electricity?" he asked in surprise.

"No, when it closed down it was one of the last lighthouses to still use oil."

With long, gentle fingers, he turned to the next blank page while she continued to hold the book.

"Since you're the new owner, maybe your name should be next."

Emily liked the idea, but she had no right. She shook her head. "My name doesn't belong there."

"You're saving the lighthouse, aren't you?"

"It's not the same thing."

He was quiet a moment. "No, I suppose not."

She closed the book and returned it to its place of honor. Then she turned around, expecting Sonny to step back, but he didn't.

With just a few inches separating them, she looked up into his thoughtful eyes. "Thank you," she whispered. "You've given me the most wonderful gift."

"You're welcome, Mrs. Maxwell." His arms encircled her and he pulled her close. She'd never been pressed against a man like this. They were touching from chest to knee. She could feel the sinewy hardness of his body through their layers of clothing. Her breath caught. Her heart began to hammer madly.

One hand was splayed against her lower spine, pressing gently, coaxing her even nearer. His other hand came up. With his forefinger, he gently traced her bottom lip.

"You're so beautiful," he breathed.

Her lips parted on a sigh.

His head came down and his mouth replaced his finger. His lips moved across hers. Slowly...gently...

She felt hot and cold and dizzy all at the same time.

But even though her body weakened, her mind picked up niggling doubts. She'd married Sonny because she thought he needed her, because she loved him. On the other hand, he'd married her be-cause...because...

He'd married her out of a sense of chivalry.

She wanted more from him. She wanted love.

Panic grew. She pushed at his chest. "Sonny—"

His mouth was on her arched throat, doing won-derful things. Things she had to stop. "Sonny—"

"Mmm?"

"Sonny—I— Please—stop."

Her words finally sunk in. With his arms still encir-cling her waist, he pulled away enough to look down at her. His lips were a little red, his eyes dark with de-sire. A frown creased his usually smooth brow.

"Emily, I know we haven't discussed this, but I'd never force you into something you didn't want."

His voice, his wonderful deep voice, seemed even deeper than usual. It reverberated against her chest.

Her heart.

"Some guys expect payment for things. But I want you to know I'm not like that. You don't owe me any-thing," he said. "I bought the lighthouse because I wanted to give it to you. It's as simple as that. I mar-ried you to save your reputation. What I'm saying is, I didn't do it to get in your bed, okay? If you want separate bedrooms, I'll respect that decision."

Was he waiting for her to answer yes or no? Emily could feel her face burning. This was embarrassing, confusing, humiliating.

"Thanks for being so understanding," she said a little grudgingly. He could have taken it a bit harder. After all, he was supposed to be swept away by passion, not stand there telling her he could take her or leave her, it made no difference.

And why not? After all the beautiful women he'd known, she could only disappoint him. No, she wouldn't disappoint him. To be disappointed, you have to expect something. He obviously expected nothing.

That night, Emily lay in bed, staring blankly at the ceiling. It was a long time before she heard Sonny make his way to the bedroom across the hall. It was a lot longer time before Emily fell asleep.

The next morning she slipped into a pair of pinwale corduroys and a bulky fisherman's sweater. As she dressed, she was aware of the silence in the house and was sure Sonny had left.

She checked his room. His bed was made. It looked so fresh she wondered if it had been slept in at all.

She finally found him outside, on the leeward side of the cottage, planting a garden.

He had spaded up approximately a ten-by-twelve-foot section of earth. It was perfectly straight, the edges lying parallel to the house. He'd already worked the dirt smooth, and was now on his knees, planting onions in the furrow he'd made with a hoe.

It was quite obvious that he'd never planted a garden before. He was planting the onions upside down.

It was hard for her to grasp the fact that a chore so much a part of her life could be entirely new to someone else.

He seemed so earnest that she hardly had the heart to tell him he was doing it wrong.

She made a nervous sound with her throat. "So...
you're planting a garden."

He glanced up, then back at his work. "Yep."

She pressed a finger to her lips, wondering what to
do. Men didn't like being told they were doing something wrong. It wounded their pride.

But the onions wouldn't grow that way.

Finally she gave up and said, "You're planting them
upside down."

"What?"

"The onions. You're planting them upside down."

The air was crisp, but the sun was warm, holding a
promise of a beautiful day. The sweet scent of freshly
turned earth drifted to her on the morning breeze.

Sonny leaned back on his heels, then looked up
from the garden to her. "No kidding?"

"No kidding."

She stepped around the spaded ground to kneel beside him in the grass. She picked up an onion from the
furrow. "This pointed end," she showed him, "is the
top. The flat end is the bottom." She tucked it in the
ground the way it should be.

"What do you know."

No anger. Just a kind of childlike amazement.

She'd loved him that day in his cabin, when he'd
asked her to marry him and she'd turned down his
proposal. But it wasn't until now that she began to realize the full magnitude of that love.

And it scared her.

They hadn't spoken of the future, but she knew with sudden certainty that if he left she would never be the same.

The garden didn't mean he planned to stay, she warned herself. Onions didn't take long to grow. In just a couple of weeks a person could use the long green shoots in salads.

After the onions, they planted leaf lettuce and spinach—both short-season crops. But then Sonny pulled a package of snap beans from the pocket of his hip-length denim jacket. Snap beans, on the other hand, took about six weeks.

She helped him plant them, helped to make it *their* garden, their hands intermingling as they covered seeds and smoothed dirt. When they were done, he presented her with another packet, this one zinnia seeds.

Grasping the tiny packet in both hands, she looked up at him. "Flowers?"

He shrugged. "I saw them and thought they might be nice."

A man who planted flowers valued beauty for its own sake. He was so special, so very special.

His last package contained cantaloupe seeds.

"But Sonny," she said, "cantaloupe takes about four months to mature."

The eyes that looked up at her were clear. "I'm in no hurry."

Their life together settled into an easy routine. Instead of returning to his work on the mainland, Sonny decided to take some time off to work on their new home. In the mornings, when the dew was still on the ground and fog still clung to the low spots, Sonny would walk Emily to her shop. Then he would return to the lighthouse and spend the day repairing and painting.

On her first day back at work, Sonny surprised her by showing up at noon with a sack lunch which they shared in the tiny shop among bolts of fabrics and the smell of glue. He took an interest in her work, making a few helpful suggestions. In the evening, he sometimes came to help her bring in the kite.

And so the pattern of their days seemed to be set. Barely a week had passed and the townspeople were already adjusting to Sonny's presence in their small community. They were simple people, much more impressed by the work Sonny was doing on the lighthouse than by how many covers his face had looked out from.

If any tourist happened to catch sight of him, they thought the man in the faded jeans and sweatshirt was simply someone who looked like Sonny Maxwell. And Sonny had been right about the press losing interest in a married man. So far, no one had bothered him, possibly because the nation's attention was now focused on a smutty political scandal.

One evening when the sky had turned orange and the air was still warm from the sun's rays, Emily came home to find Babbie and Sonny painting the ornate railing that surrounded the porch. Neither one had heard Emily approach, so engrossed were they in their work.

Emily was loath to break up their comradery so she stood with her hand poised on the gate. Babbie chattered incessantly, obviously feeling quite proud and adult at being allowed to help. Occasionally Sonny would toss out a comment, his voice so low and deep that Emily couldn't hear what he said.

Then, without thinking, Babbie ran up the porch steps, her paintbrush dripping white on the gray enamel. When she realized what she'd done, she stood there, her face a study in horror and anguish, staring at the white globs. Then her little mouth began to tremble, and her eyes filled with tears.

"Easy now—" Sonny grabbed a rag and quickly wiped up the spills. "All fixed," he announced. Then he dried Babbie's tears and helped her to blow her nose.

And Emily's love for Sonny grew.

The following Saturday they had an unexpected visitor. Emily answered a loud knock to find Doreen standing at the door. Fear jumped in Emily's chest. To her, Doreen symbolized Sonny's work, Sonny's real life, the place he belonged.

Why else would she be here, if not to coax him back, to coax him away from her?

"I can't stay long," Doreen announced, stepping in the door. "Ferry leaves in two hours. I just had to see how you kids were doing. And I brought Sonny's mail." She let her briefcase slip from her fingers to the floor with a heavy thud.

With hardly a pause, she crossed the room and stopped directly in front of the black-and-white photo of the lighthouse that used to hang in Sonny's cabin.

"What a wonderful photo," Doreen said, awe in her voice. "I don't believe I recognize the work." She peered at the corner, searching for a signature.

"It's Sonny's. He took it," Emily said.

Doreen swung around, surprise in her face. "Sonny?" She looked back at the photo. "Yes... I can see Sonny there. The boy's been holding out on me. I'd have arranged a showing for him."

She seemed a little hurt. Emily felt the need to explain. "He's just so private."

"Secretive, that's what he is," Doreen said.

"Yes."

The sadness she couldn't seem to keep from her voice caught Doreen's attention.

"One thing you have to realize is that emotionally, Sonny is a child," Doreen said. "It's going to take time to undo the damage his mother caused."

"His mother?" Sonny had never mentioned any family to her.

"He'll probably never say anything to you about it, but you're his wife. You have a right to know. Sonny didn't have the silver spoon childhood everybody thinks he had. Not that I'm an authority on his past, I'm not. No one is. All I know is that he was raised in a boardinghouse for child actors. The place was eventually closed down because of cruelty and unsanitary living conditions. But not until Sonny had spent ten years of his life there. People have always thought of him as the kid who was spoiled rotten, as the kid who had everything. The truth is, he had nothing. He was a commodity, nothing more."

Everything fell into place. The dark colors Emily sometimes felt around him, the aloofness. She hurt for him. Ached for him.

Oh, Sonny.

Some of what she was feeling must have shown on her face, because Doreen said, "For God's sake, don't pity him. He hates that." She looked at her watch. "Speaking of Sonny...?"

"He's working on the lighthouse."

"Working, as in manual labor? This," Doreen said, hitching her camera strap more securely on her shoulder, "I've got to see."

As they approached the lighthouse, they could see Sonny in the distance, hammering on the wooden walkway that led to the lighthouse. He was wearing a dirt-smudged white T-shirt, faded jeans and tennis shoes. A breeze ruffled his sun-kissed hair.

Love, aching and sweet, filled Emily. She hoped in her heart to somehow make up for the desolate years of his life.

"I've got to get a picture of this," Doreen said, stopping to dig out her camera. "Nobody will ever believe it."

Emily didn't need to be reminded of the fact that Sonny didn't belong here. She thought about it every day.

She hugged her arms to her and watched her husband while the camera shutter clicked beside her. She would knit him a sweater, she thought. Blue-gray, to match his eyes. It would be a secret, a surprise.

Doreen stuck the camera back in her bag, then waved her arm and hooted at Sonny.

He looked up. As soon as he saw them, he put down the hammer and came toward them.

"God! You look so domestic," Doreen said. "It's disgusting."

He smiled. "I never expected to see you here. The way you griped when we were doing the shoot."

"I can tolerate fresh air in small doses. Anyway, I brought your mail. People are hounding me, wanting to know when you're coming back. Carrie Ivy from *Elite Magazine* wants you to do this thing in Ireland. What should I tell her?"

"Tell her, no thanks. Tell her I'm taking a long vacation."

"The American public has a short attention span. If you're out of the public eye for too long, somebody else will come along and take your place."

Sonny took her heavy camera case and slung it over one shoulder. "How 'bout some lunch?"

While Sonny was in the bathroom washing up, Doreen helped Emily put some sandwiches together.

It was nice, sitting in the warm sunny kitchen, talking over coffee and sandwiches. Doreen didn't mention the magazine article again, apparently knowing that Sonny had meant what he said.

An hour later, Doreen glanced at her watch. "I better be on my way. It's been fun."

"Before you go, come and have a look at our garden," Sonny said.

Every day he checked their garden, just like Babbie. It had been planted two weeks ago, and everything was pushing through the dirt already.

After Doreen admired the garden, they strolled around the yard, Sonny pointing out various improvements he'd made. At one point, when he was out of earshot, Doreen took Emily by the arm and pulled her close. "He's changed," she whispered.

"Changed?" That fear again. And Emily wondered if it would always be like this, if there would ever be any settledness to her love for Sonny.

"I don't know if I'd go so far as to call it contentment, but it's close to that. I've never seen Sonny content. It looks good on him."

They walked Doreen to her rental car, then stood and waved until its tail lights disappeared over the dandelion-covered hill that led to the village.

Emily turned to find Sonny studying the freshly painted house with quiet satisfaction. Doreen was right. He did seem content.

"You like it here, don't you?" she asked.

All along, she'd been dreading the time when he became tired of living on St. Genevieve. All along she'd been thinking there was nothing here he would want, that this was transient.

But on St. Genevieve, there was peace. On St. Genevieve, a person could plant a garden, and repair a lighthouse. On St. Genevieve, there was someone who loved him.

His gaze drifted past the lighthouse, past the blue, blue ocean to finally settle on her. "Yes," he said quietly. "I like it here."

It wasn't much. But from Sonny, it was a lot.

Good things took time. Like Sonny and his garden, Emily could wait.

Chapter Eight

Sonny stood on the beach, hands in the front pockets of the gray dress pants he'd worn to church. The sun was warm on his face, the salt wind cool as it whipped the hair back from his brow.

He tried not to think too deeply about the turn his life had taken. Not that he was superstitious. He just didn't want to take any chances.

He knew it was crazy, but he was afraid if he consciously thought about how happy he was, some higher order would pick up on his thoughts and take it all away.

And there was one thing he was sure of. He wasn't ready for it to end. Maybe his concern had to do with the fact that he'd done nothing to deserve this. He'd done nothing to deserve Emily.

Shrieks of laughter drew his gaze down the long stretch of beach. Emily and her sisters were making their way toward him, looking for treasures as they went, playing tag with the waves and laughing whenever the water swirled about their bare ankles.

They had invited him to walk the beach with them, but he'd declined, knowing he had to keep some distance, had to hold back. He couldn't allow himself to become completely caught up in their lives.

Watching them now, the scene before him brought back something he'd completely forgotten about.

He'd been about seven or eight, shooting an ad for kids' clothes. The film crew had run into some technical problems. To keep Sonny out of the way, he'd been stuck in a dressing room where he was told to wait until someone came for him.

The dressing room was hardly more than a closet with peeling paint and bare pipes and no heat. But on one wall was a huge print of an oil painting—the kind of cheap print that was sold in dime stores, warped frame and all.

Maybe it had been hung to cover a hole, he didn't know. It didn't matter. It was the faded picture that fascinated him.

It was a turn-of-the-century painting of a woman and two children. They were strolling on the beach, the woman wearing a long flowing dress, holding a ruffled parasol over one shoulder. The children were dressed in the striped bathing suits people wore back then.

Looking at the picture made him feel good, and it made him feel bad. It made him feel lonely, made him ache for something he couldn't define, something obscure and unattainable.

The film crew apparently forgot about him, because Sonny ended up sitting in the room for hours, staring at the picture, wishing he could step inside the frame and become a part of it.

Now, watching Emily and her sisters, he felt the same ache he'd felt that day looking at the painting, that same yearning.

But he knew he could no more be a part of their lives than he could have stepped into that painting all those years ago. He'd been a kid then. Now he was old enough to know that there were barriers that couldn't be transcended. One was physical; the other emotional.

He wanted what he had here with Emily to be real. He wanted it to be forever. But it couldn't be. Because he wasn't who she thought he was, he wasn't who anybody thought he was.

Sonny was afraid of the day Emily would look deep into his soul with those magic eyes of hers, and see him, *really* see him.

A pretty package with nothing inside.

And she would see that he wasn't completely real, because to be real, you had to be a part of life. But that's the way he liked it, he reminded himself. That's the way he wanted it.

So he watched, as he'd always watched, on the outside looking in.

He watched as Babbie extended her hand to Tilly, showing her something. Sonny used to think kids were kids. But now, looking at the girls, he was struck by how different they were from one another. Tilly...she was something—a regular tomboy. As soon as she'd gotten home from church, she'd torn off her dress and replaced it with jeans, T-shirt, and high-top sneakers. Claire, on the other hand was still wearing her church clothes. Whenever she thought no one was looking, she'd spin in a circle, watching her dress swirl about her.

And then there was Babbie.... The child was disarmingly open and trusting, completely guileless. Like Emily.

Emily.

He must have said her name in his mind a thousand times. Sweet, sweet Emily. She took his breath away. She filled him with a longing. And she made him feel things he hadn't felt since childhood, things he'd never thought to feel again, things that weren't safe to feel.

As he watched her, a smile tugged at the corners of his mouth, and sweet sadness touched his heart. She looked like a sea nymph, a mermaid. The wind teased her. It played with her tangled blond hair, it lifted the hem of her skirt, allowing him tantalizing glimpses of long, slim legs.

When they were together at the cottage, he liked to watch the graceful way she moved around the house. And even if they weren't in the same room, he liked knowing she was nearby. He would find himself waiting for her soft footstep, listening, hoping to hear her humming softly to herself the way she sometimes did.

It felt so right.

Having grown up with weak roots, with people wandering in one door of his life and out the other, it hardly occurred to him that their life together could possibly be permanent.

Yes, it was going to be hard to leave here. Maybe the hardest thing he'd ever done.

"Sonny! Sonny!"

Babbie.

Her voice pulled his thoughts back to the beach, the sand, the sun, to the child hurrying toward him as fast as her short legs could go.

"Look what I found!" she said in breathless excitement, her Irish eyes shining as only Babbie's Irish eyes could shine.

Sonny crouched down in front of her.

"It's a house," she announced, shoving a shell under his nose.

He drew his head back enough to see the pointed conch shell held in her small, chubby hand. "A house?" he asked, baffled. He'd been around Babbie enough times to know that her mind didn't function like his. It was best to wait and let her explain.

"A house for Herman Crab."

She pointed one finger at the shell's opening. "He's scared of us, so he's hiding in there."

Her voice dropped, as if she'd just reminded herself of the creature's fear. "Emily said if I'm quiet, maybe he'll come out." She plopped herself down on the sand to wait, shell cradled in the palm of both hands.

Tilly and Claire dashed breathlessly toward them, scattering dry sand as they fell to their knees. They dumped the treasures they'd collected near their pile of shoes.

"Did you show Sonny your hermit crab?" Tilly asked.

"Herman," Babbie insisted. "His name is *Herman*. Herman Crab."

Tilly rolled her eyes. "Oh, brother." She leaned toward Sonny, pointing a thumb at her younger sister. "She's always getting words mixed up. She says the weirdest stuff."

Claire daintily shook sand from her skirt. "You shouldn't be talking, Tilly. What about *you*?"

"I don't say weird stuff."

"Oh, yes you do. What about the time Emily asked you to take those kites to the church bazaar and leave them on the miscellaneous table?"

Tilly's eyes snapped. "Shut up," she warned.

Claire started laughing uncontrollably. Her face turned red and her eyes filled with tears as she struggled to relate the story to Sonny. "Hours later, she came back with the kites and said...and said..." She doubled over and clutched her stomach, gasping for air. "She said she couldn't find anybody named *Miss* Alaneous!" The sentence was spewed out in one long burst, then Claire collapsed in a hysterical heap.

"Quit laughing!" Tilly shrieked, her face red with rage. She dove for her sister. Sonny lunged, grabbing

Tilly around the waist, holding her so that her arms flailed at nothing but air.

"Stop!" Babbie wailed. "You're scaring Herman! Now he'll never come out!"

Sonny was at a complete loss. He'd never been in the middle of such a squabble, such noise. He'd never had to deal with a bunch of fighting girls.

"Emily!" he shouted, frantic. He scanned the beach and was relieved to see her hurrying in their direction.

"What's wrong?" Her gaze flitted from one to the other, inspecting them all for injuries. "Is somebody hurt?"

"I *wish*!" Tilly said through gritted teeth, taking another swing in the direction of the now smirking Claire.

"She's making fun of me!" Tilly shouted.

"I only told Sonny about the time Tilly spent all afternoon looking for someone named *Miss* Alaneous!"

Emily's hand went to her mouth in an attempt to hide her own smile. But Sonny could see the sparkle of it in her blue eyes. Then her shoulders began to shake.

"Now *everybody's* laughing at me!" Tilly squirmed out of Sonny's grip, glared at them all, one at a time, then stomped off—as well as she could in the loose sand.

Sonny started to go after her.

"Let her go." Emily lay a hand on his arm. "Tilly always has to have the upper hand. When she doesn't, she gets mad. She heats up fast, but she cools down fast, too. In five minutes, she'll have forgotten all about it."

"I'm going to feed the birds." Claire grabbed up the plastic bag of bread she'd brought and flounced off.

"Claire, on the other hand," Emily said as she watched her sister make her way down the beach, "keeps things inside. She can stay mad at somebody for a month."

They watched as Claire tossed bits of bread to the hovering gulls.

Two minutes later, Tilly joined her. Claire held out the open bread sack. Tilly reached inside. Soon they were both laughing and tossing crumbs, friends again.

Sonny shook his head. "Amazing."

"I don't know if there's any truth to it," Emily said, "But child psychologists claim that sibling rivalry teaches children to deal with people in later life. It would be easier to tolerate their fighting if I knew they were gaining something from it."

"If it *is* true, then Claire and Tilly should grow up to be a couple of well-adjusted adults," Sonny observed dryly.

Emily turned to look directly at him, surprise on her face. And it occurred to him that he'd never teased her before.

Then she smiled. The sun reflected in her eyes, shimmering in the flaxen curls of her windblown hair. He decided right then and there that he would have to make her smile more often.

Sonny knew that the press portrayed him as a hot sexual dynamo who was always on the prowl. He'd read interviews by women he'd never met who claimed he'd made mad, passionate love to them all night and all day.

He couldn't deny that he had normal urges. But he was nothing like the press made him out to be. Sexual encounters usually left him feeling unsatisfied, even used. It hadn't taken him long to realize that they wanted the personified Sonny Maxwell, and once they'd found him, he was simply a trophy, a notch on their bedpost.

During an interview he was once asked what it was about him that made women go wild. Sonny answered, saying it was everything he *wasn't* that attracted them. The interviewer hadn't understood.

His encounters with women had left a bitter mark. It had been years since he had wanted to touch someone for the sake of touching them.

Until now. Until Emily.

At times like these, when Emily was so close, it was as if he could feel himself tumbling headlong into the blueness of her eyes. He felt as if she could see into his mind and heart and was coaxing him to take that step.

She stood there watching him in that quiet, unsettling way of hers. Then, as she watched, her smile faded, became a little unsure. Her pink lips trembled slightly. Lips he knew would be soft, would open sweetly under his.

He struggled to shut down his thoughts, shut down his feelings, pull away—something that used to be so easy. But with Emily...things were different. They no longer followed the same time-tested patterns. He couldn't understand.

He wasn't a toucher.

And yet a hundred times a day he had to stop himself from touching her.

Right now he wanted to touch her face, her hair, her hands. He wanted to pull her into his arms and touch his lips to hers. He wanted to feel the softness of her hair slide through his fingers. He wanted to feel the warmth of her skin against his.

But he wasn't a toucher.

So why did he want to touch Emily?

You love her, a voice in his head taunted.

Love?

No.

Denial roared through him.

It wasn't true. Couldn't be true.

You didn't marry her out of a sense of chivalry. You married her because you need her.

Over the past weeks, he'd been distantly aware of a change going on inside him, a change he had up until now tried to ignore. A softening, a crumbling of his defenses. But emotions long suppressed were fighting their way to the surface, coming closer and closer.

No.

He didn't need anybody.

Sweat broke out on his forehead. Fear scuttled through him, running rampant, pounding like a madman to get out.

He'd always been so careful. There had been so many women who had desired him, but he'd had no trouble brushing them aside.

But Emily... Oh God. Sweet, sweet Emily. With her magic.

Her name was a sigh in his mind. Sweet, sweet Emily, with eyes the color of the ocean, eyes the color of the sky, eyes that seemed to look right into his heart.

Then it hit him, and the shock was like a blow: He was no longer on the outside looking in.

He denied it vehemently.

No.

Through a fog, he felt her small fingers brush the back of his hand, felt them curl against his palm, gently squeezing his fingers, just as he had the day of their wedding when he'd seen her fear and felt the need to reassure her.

His throat tightened. The wind burned his eyes.

Lord, what have I done?

Behind them, Babbie's little girl voice whispered, "Hello, Herman."

Chapter Nine

Emily watched the tortured expressions flit across Sonny's face. She sensed his withdrawal.

He's leaving me, she realized with shock. She could see it in his eyes.

She was still holding his hand and now he pulled away, slipping free of her light grasp.

Her heart hammered. Her mind raced, frantically seeking an answer. What could she possibly say or do to make him stay? What had she done to make him decide to go?

He couldn't leave. She loved him.

She'd have told herself she could wait for him forever—if that's what it took. But she couldn't wait for someone who wasn't there.

More than anything, she wanted to open her heart, she wanted to tell him that she loved him—in so many ways. She wanted to tell him she loved him for all the pain he kept locked deep inside. That she loved him for walking with her on misty mornings; she loved him for his patience with Babbie; for taking sad, soulful pictures that made her want to cry.

For planting flowers.

But she knew he wasn't ready to hear those words from her. With something too much like grief, she realized he might never be ready.

Sonny.

He had so many colors in him. She had wanted to be the one to touch his heart and set those colors free.

She'd taken his hand, offered her friendship and comfort and he'd rejected her. In her whole sheltered existence, she'd never felt the sting of rejection.

It hurt.

She thought about Sonny, the child, growing up a commodity, left in the hands of uncaring strangers. How had he stood it? He'd stood it by building a wall, a fortress that was now possibly too big and too solid for anyone to tear down.

She turned away so he couldn't see the pain in her eyes—pain for him, pain for her. She called to the girls, telling them it was time to go, telling them she would walk them home.

They put on their shoes, then gathered their treasures. Babbie returned Herman to the spot she'd found him. They started to walk away but stopped when Sonny gave no indication that he was coming with them. Emily paused and waited.

"Go on without me," he said, standing with his hands in his pockets, the salt wind lifting his hair. The remote look was still in his eyes. "I'll see you later."

She thought about the sweater she was knitting. The sleeves were almost done. She had planned to start on the back soon. The yarn matched his eyes perfectly, having been dyed with the gray-blue flowers that grew wild on St. Genevieve. Who would wear the sweater now? She knew of no one else with eyes the color of a stormy sea.

"I'll see you later," she said.

He nodded.

She felt it in her heart, saw it in his face. It was over. This game they'd played, the pretending. But all the while they had been pretending, she'd cherished a hope that it would grow to be more, that it would eventually grow to become real.

With her sisters beside her, she turned and headed up the sand dune to the path that led to her father's house.

After seeing the girls settled, Emily started home. The solitude of her walk was in stark contrast to the trip to church that morning. Earlier, her heart had felt light. Earlier, Sonny had been by her side.

She kept replaying the afternoon in her mind, trying to make sense of what had happened, what she had said or done that had caused him to retreat the way he had.

There could be no mistaking the trapped look she'd seen in his eyes. Sonny, who was so good at hiding his emotions, had come close to falling apart in front of her.

When she reached the cottage, Sonny wasn't there, but she hadn't really expected him to be. She changed into her soft corduroy pants and a pullover sweater. Then she went through the motions of fixing supper. She set the table, then sat down and waited.

He didn't come.

She put the food away untouched and returned the plates to the cupboard.

She pushed aside the kitchen curtain. Darkness had fallen. A single glimmer of light could be seen coming from the small lighthouse window.

So, that's where he was.

It was a fitting place for him. He spent a lot of time there; he seemed drawn to it. And in a way, they were alike, the lighthouse and Sonny. Strong and alone, wrapped in their solitude.

Hadn't she done all she could do? But for every step closer she'd taken, he'd taken two away. Sonny was like a prisoner who had spent most of his life behind bars and was afraid to be set free.

She longed to go to him, to talk with him, but he was making it quite clear that he wanted to be alone. She must respect that.

She curled up at one end of the couch, tucking her feet under her. They hadn't gotten a television, both agreeing that it was unnecessary. But now Emily thought she would have welcomed the distraction.

Perhaps what bothered her most about all of this was the sudden realization that she was no closer to him now than she had been that day he'd pulled her from the water. It seemed as if she had breached one wall, only to find there were hundreds more on the other side.

She wished he would trust her, share himself with her. He thought she didn't know him, but she did. He didn't have to tell her his deepest thoughts in order for her to know who he was. His inner self came through in a thousand different ways.

Time passed. She must have drifted off to sleep. She awoke all of a sudden, her head lying against her arm at an uncomfortable angle, a cramp in her neck. She sat there awhile, disoriented from falling asleep in a place other than her bed.

A flash of lightning lit the room, and she realized just why she'd awakened so suddenly. Thunder rolled in across the ocean, echoing off the rocky shore, rattling the glass in the windowpanes. The wind howled. Somewhere in the house a shutter banged.

The first thing she did was hurry to Sonny's room and flick on the light. His bed was still empty.

Rain poured in the open window. She crossed the room, closed the window and secured the shutter, her thoughts on Sonny.

Was he all right? What if he was hurt? What if he'd slipped on a wet step? What if he'd fallen and hit his head?

Coming to a decision, she hurried through the sitting room and out the front door.

Wind tugged at her hair. Rain slashed her face as she stepped from the porch, the unexpected chill of it driving the breath from her lungs.

Aided by the occasional flash of lightning, she ran up the slippery wooden walkway to the lighthouse. Fingers wet and stiff with cold, she felt for the latch, found it and pushed open the door to stumble into the small, circular room.

There was no electricity in the lighthouse. Hanging from a metal hook embedded in the stone wall was a hurricane lamp, its flame casting shadows across the small, tidy room.

Sonny hadn't heard her come in, the sound of her entrance obviously drowned out by the storm. He was standing at the casement window, his back to her, watching the light show nature was performing over the crashing waves.

He'd changed clothes. Instead of the gray dress slacks, he was wearing a ragged sweatshirt and jeans.

"Sonny."

She barely spoke above a whisper, but he turned toward her, one hand resting on the wide stone sill of the window.

"Emily."

His low, deep voice seemed a part of the rumbling thunder, blending with the storm. His eyes still held the remoteness she'd seen on the beach, their barren depths chilling her more than the rain could ever do.

Don't do this to me. Don't pull away like this. She'd been so careful not to intrude on his space, been so careful to give him the distance he needed.

"What are you doing here?" he asked. It seemed as if he struggled to pull his thoughts together—as if her presence in the lighthouse confused him. Maybe because in his mind, he'd already left her.

"I was worried about you," she said.

"You shouldn't have come out in the storm. I'm a big boy. I can take care of myself."

Can you, Sonny? Can you take care of yourself?

Not waiting for an invitation that might never come she crossed the room to join him at the window, the wet soles of her tennis shoes making tiny squeaking sounds on the flagstone.

She peered through the rain and sea-spattered glass. The electronic beacon was doing its job, cutting a bright path through the rain, its light reflecting off the water, the clouds.

"When they first put the buoy out there," she said in a desperate attempt to make conversation, to draw him back to her, "my grandfather said a part of him died." With one finger, she drew in the condensation on the window. A droplet formed, then trickled down the glass like a tear. "At first, he didn't trust it. At night, he couldn't sleep for fear the light might go out."

"Did it ever go out?" Sonny asked, sounding truly interested.

"No. I really think my grandfather wanted it to. I think he needed to know that he couldn't be replaced so easily. I think he felt that the buoy made a mockery of his life."

Sonny sighed. "Everybody's replaceable. It's a sad truth nobody wants to hear."

She turned to him, watching his profile as he stared out at the churning water. "You don't really believe that, do you?"

"Yeah. Don't you?"

"No. No, I don't."

He shrugged, as if to say he knew better and there was no sense in arguing.

"How can you say that?" she asked. "Look at all the lives you've touched."

He turned—and it shocked her to see the ravage of the years reflected in his young eyes.

"It doesn't count," he said, "unless they've been touched in a positive way."

What had put such darkness in his heart? She was afraid it was her, afraid it was something she'd done, something she'd said. "You're thinking of leaving, aren't you?" she asked.

He made an odd sound, half amused, half pained. "There you go, mermaid. Reading my mind. I always knew you were magic."

"So, you *are* leaving..."

"You have to look at it from my angle," he said. There was a forced lightness to his voice, a stiffness in his posture. "I'm not used to staying in one place for very long."

It was an excuse. She knew it. "I'm not magic," she said. "But I wish I were." If so, she would use her power to make him stay.

"Oh, you're magic, all right," he whispered. "You've cast a spell on me."

"A spell?" She was unable to stop the beginning of a smile, glad that the conversation was getting lighter. She hated to see him sad. "What kind of spell?"

The distance was gone from his eyes. He was looking at her, really seeing her. And then, with his deep voice breaking a little, "I want you like I've never wanted anybody before."

Oh my.

In the same instant Emily was struck dumb with wonder, a jagged knife of lightning struck something very close to the lighthouse, a flash of brilliant light illuminating the tiny room. A breath later, thunder rattled the windows and sent shuddering echoes through Emily's chest. Out on the open water, sparks flew.

It took Emily a few seconds to fully grasp what had happened.

Lightning had struck the electronic buoy.

Chapter Ten

Like Fourth of July fireworks, a shower of sparks arched skyward, then slowly drifted down to hit the water, sizzling out. When it was over, Emily strained her eyes, but the spot where the buoy was anchored was now bathed in total darkness.

"My God!" A multitude of disjointed thoughts raced through her brain. Must get help...call coast guard...get to a phone...it could be hours before help came.... A boat could be passing anytime, a boat could be passing *right now*—

Sonny's voice broke through the confusion in her mind. "Is there someone on the island—someone responsible for the light?"

"No." She swallowed, the implications of what had happened sinking in little by little. "The coast guard only comes by for routine maintenance. There isn't anybody. Even if we used Papa's phone, it will be hours before anybody gets here. Maybe dawn."

She knew it was wrong, but beneath the horror of the moment, Emily felt a quiet hurrah for her grandfather. His life *had* mattered.

"We have to do something," Sonny said. He grabbed her by both arms and swung her around to face him. "You said you used to come here when you were little. Did you ever watch your grandfather light the lamps?"

"All the time. He let me help him."

"Do you remember how to do it?"

"Yes. It's very simple—"

Before the last word left her mouth, Sonny was urging her in the direction of the iron staircase that led to the tower room. They ran up the stairs, with Sonny leading the way, the hurricane lamp held high, its glow casting bobbing shadows on the white stone walls.

When they reached the trapdoor, he quickly passed the lantern to Emily. He had some trouble with the iron latch, finally managing to swing the door open with a crash of metal against metal.

Sonny disappeared through the small square opening. Emily followed.

As soon as she felt the metal of the tower floor beneath her feet, she rushed to the nearest lamp and unscrewed the lid. The wick was still in place and smelling of oil, but the lamp was empty. She hurried to another one, with Sonny doing likewise.

"They're all empty," he said, his voice echoing in the small chamber. "Would there be any oil someplace else?"

"I don't think so. It used to be kept in drums downstairs. But they aren't even there anymore."

She squeezed her eyes shut in frustration. What would her grandfather do if he were here?

Suddenly a memory came to her, like a scene taken from a movie, vivid in clarity. Her grandfather was standing beside the white cellar door. Flowers—red tulips, grew nearby.

"I always keep some oil put away," he said. "My emergency supply."

The cellar. Her eyes flew open. "The cellar. There might be oil in the cellar."

Emily waited in the dark tower while Sonny went to check the cellar. What seemed like hours later, but in reality must have been but a matter of minutes, he returned, his hair plastered to his head, his clothes soaked. But under one arm he held a dusty, five-gallon drum.

While they filled the lamps, Emily periodically cast a glance out across the water, straining her eyes to detect any small glimmer of light that might indicate a boat or ship. But each time she looked she saw nothing but darkness. Luck seemed to be on their side. Or maybe her grandfather was smiling down on them.

In a tiny cupboard Emily found the long wooden matches her grandfather had once used. She was ready to strike one when she felt Sonny place a restraining hand on her arm. "Go downstairs while I light them."

She hesitated.

"Emily—it could be dangerous."

"I have to do it. I want to do it. Don't you see?" She was the lighthouse keeper's granddaughter, carrying on the flame. She had to be the one to light it.

Sonny was watching her closely. "Okay," he finally said.

Thank you for understanding, she told him with her eyes.

He smiled and nodded.

She struck the match and held it to the first lamp. The wick hadn't quite absorbed enough oil yet, but it finally caught.

She'd never thought to again feel the excitement and wonder she'd experienced as a child when her grandfather had lifted her up so she could light the flame, a flame that would guide people she would never see, never know. But it was in her again. That reverent sense of awe.

Together, she and Sonny filled and lit the remaining lamps, ten in all. When they were done, Emily looked through the thick tower glass, past the protective iron bars.

A path of light cut across the churning water. How could ten small flames create so much light? The concave reflectors multiplied each flame by at least fifty times, creating the approximate equivalent of five hundred candlepower.

Wondrous. Magic.

And she and Sonny were standing right in the middle of all that brilliance.

They looked at each other. His hair and clothes were rain-soaked.

She smiled.

He smiled, a little drunkenly almost. And she knew how he felt. She felt the same way.

The scent of his damp skin and rain-kissed hair drifted to her. She didn't know how he managed it, but standing there soaking wet, Sonny still managed to maintain an elegance. He wasn't huge biceps and rippling muscles. He was lean and smooth. Perfect symmetry.

With her senses fully focused on him, she could feel his light. He exuded a spiritual purity that was at odds with his strong sexuality.

It occurred to her that the light in the tower was Sonny's light.

"We did it," she said, her voice level, at odds with the firestorm going on inside her.

Outside, rain beat against the glass, thunder rumbled and the wind howled.

His hands were somehow on her waist. "We did it," he said. He pulled her closer. His eyes reflected the light around them, plus something new, something that an hour ago would have seemed impossible: joy.

"Have you ever been kissed in the center of a white hot flame?" he asked.

Her breath caught. "No."

She watched him, mesmerized. "Have you?" Her voice was no longer level. It trembled.

"Not until now."

She didn't question. She didn't dare tempt the Fates.

She only prayed he wouldn't draw away, wouldn't disappear the way Sonny so often disappeared.

He didn't.

He pulled her closer. She could feel his fingers pressing against her scalp, his hand supporting her head.

"I want you—" he said, his eyes shining with rare intensity, the words seeming to have been torn from deep inside him, spoken with something near anguish.

And then suddenly, wondrously, his lips were on hers. He was kissing her with desperation, as if it might be their last kiss. His hands were everywhere. Fingers skimming her face, lacing through her hair, sliding beneath the hem of her sweater, his rough-smooth palm kneading her skin.

She clung to his arms, feeling the play of sinewy muscles beneath his damp shirt.

And the white hot flame was inside her.

The combination of passions, too long suppressed, vibrated around them, seeming to overpower the very brilliance of the room.

"Emily..." He groaned against her lips. "I want to touch you. I want to taste you. I want to feel you around me."

"Yes," she whispered, head tilted back. "Yes."

Together they sank to the floor, the metal surface jarringly cold—a hard reminder of where they were, who they were.

Sonny pulled away, as she'd feared he would. As she'd known he would.

He was on his knees, his face looming above her. Pain and remorse flashed in his eyes. Then he was rolling from her.

He sat with his elbows on bent knees, rib cage rising and falling, one hand over his face, trying to catch his breath, fighting for control.

"I'm sorry," he said, his voice harsh and rasping. "I can't believe I came close to taking you, right here—"

His hair had fallen forward. She couldn't see his face. Emily scooted across the floor and lay a hand on his shoulder. "Sonny, you don't need to apologize for almost making love to your wife."

"Not my wife. You."

He looked over his shoulder at her. "Oh, Lord. You don't understand."

Maybe if she'd been more versed in the ways of men and women, she could have understood. But he was right. She didn't understand. "Is it something I've done? Something I've said?"

"No. It's nothing you've done. It's you. *You*."

When she continued to stare blankly at him, he said, "I can't make love to somebody like you!"

The air seemed to leave Emily's body. She felt empty. Bereft. As if she'd just lost everything that ever mattered to her in the world.

"I'm sorry," she whispered, speaking more to herself than Sonny. Such a small thing to hurt so big. "I didn't know... didn't realize I was—" she groped for the right word, but could find none "—bothering you," she finally said.

He made a strange sound and started to move.

She didn't wait. She couldn't take any more. Without looking at him, she scrambled to her feet and hurried down the spiral stairs.

"Emily!"

His voice echoed off the stone walls. But she didn't stop. She reached the heavy wooden door, jerked it open and ran out into the darkness, into the lashing rain.

Chapter Eleven

Emily gained the security of her room, careful to close the door behind her. Mechanically she stripped off her wet clothes, put on her nightgown and crawled into bed.

Don't think, just don't think.

But it didn't do any good. She couldn't stop the thoughts that tumbled one after the other. She had married Sonny for the wrong reason. Oh, she had loved him, but he hadn't loved her. That's where her logic had gone astray. What was that grade school chant? First comes love, then comes marriage?

She had done it all backwards, hoping to make him eventually come to care for her, simply by willing it. But you can't *make* somebody love you.

Her throat felt raw, but she wouldn't cry.

She'd grown up in a world of seasons, a world where waiting was a part of life. She had thought all she had to do was wait . . . and everything would gradually fall into place.

But it hadn't happened that way.

And now he was leaving. He didn't love her. Those were the two things she must face. The lesson for today. This week's memory verse.

He's leaving. He doesn't love me.

Say it again, with more feeling this time.

He's leaving. He doesn't . . . doesn't—

From nowhere came a sob, tearing at her throat, frightening in its intensity. She wanted her father. She wanted her mother. She wanted her sisters.

She wanted Sonny.

But Sonny didn't want her.

She heard the front door open, heard quiet footsteps cross the living room.

Sonny.

Quickly she reached out and switched off the bedside lamp, tugged the covers over her shoulder and turned her back to the door. She tried to hold her breath, tried to stifle the hiccupping sobs that were coming one after the other.

She heard his footsteps in the hall, stopping in front of her closed door.

She could feel him listening.

"Emily?"

If she kept quiet, maybe he would think she was asleep. She didn't want him to know he'd made her cry. He wouldn't want to know he'd hurt her. And if he found her in tears, he'd realize just how foolish she was. He would know that she was in love with him—just like all the other silly million and one women in the world.

Behind her, the door creaked. A shaft of light crept across the room, spilling on the wall opposite her face. She was trying to breathe shallowly, but when she inhaled she made an involuntary shuddering sound.

She squeezed her eyes shut.

"Emily."

That single word carried with it a multitude of emotions. Reproach, hurt, sorrow, love.

Love? No, not love. It couldn't be love.

He must have been barefoot, because she hardly heard him as he crossed the room.

The bed creaked and dipped, but she didn't move.

"Emily...?" He was sitting behind her, on the opposite side of the bed.

"Please go away." To her further humiliation, her voice came out sounding as if she had a bad cold. Now he would know she'd been crying.

"Emily, I'm sorry. I didn't mean to hurt your feelings. I'd never hurt you intentionally. Never."

She sniffled.

He left the room, but returned almost immediately. This time he came around the bed and sat down in front of her. The bed dipped and she rolled against him, her thighs pressing against the warmth of his back.

"Emily—come here," he coaxed. "Sit up."

She didn't seem to have much willpower where Sonny was concerned. She levered herself to a sitting position, surprised to find that he had set a box of tissues on the bed. Then, as if she were no older than Babbie, he helped her dry her tears and blow her nose.

"I wanted you to like me," she mumbled, eyes downcast, staring intently at the bedspread.

"I do like you, mermaid."

Oh, the gentleness of his voice. The gentleness of his hands.

"You like me like a sister. Somebody who bothers you. Not somebody you want to... want to hold."

"You bother me all right. You bother me so much I can't sleep. You bother me so much, I can't think. When I do manage to sleep, I dream about you. I dream of touching you. I dream about holding you as close as a man can hold a woman. Whenever you're around, it's sweet torture, because I remember those dreams. Yes. Lord, yes. You bother me."

Wonderful words! "I bother you...." She chanced a peek. "Like that?"

He lay a palm against her cheek and stared into her eyes. "Like that."

Her heart was hammering madly. He dreamed about her!

"In your dreams," she whispered, reaching to touch the back of his hand with shy fingertips, "where do you touch me?"

"Everywhere."

Her breath caught. "Everywhere?"

His hand wrapped around hers. "With my hands. My mouth. My body..."

"That sounds..." because it seemed to be the word of the hour, she said, "magical."

"It is."

"Sonny...I want you to touch me the way you touch me in your dreams."

He made a tormented sound deep in his throat. "Emily—I'm trying to be strong. I don't want to hurt you any more than I already have. We can end this now and nobody will be hurt. I can leave here tomorrow."

"I don't want it to end," she said desperately. "I don't want you to leave." What had he told her all of this for, if only to end it? "The only way you can hurt me is if you turn away. Please Sonny, don't turn away."

It was going to be okay.

She could see it in his eyes. Slowly, as if afraid of startling her, he pulled her near, into his arms, against the warmth of him. His head came down and his mouth touched hers.

Cold.

Warm.

"You're so cold," he whispered, his arms tightening around her.

"You're so warm."

His lips moved over hers. Slow. Lazy. He'd kissed her before, but never so sensuously. It took her breath away, sent blood pounding to her toes and fingers.

Then she felt the wetness of his tongue slide across her lips, urging them open.

His tongue slipped inside.

Her back was pressed to the feather mattress. Then Sonny was stretching out his lean length beside her, drawing her close to his heart.

"First, I'll touch you with my hands."

He ran nimble fingers across her lips, her brow, her hair, her throat. Then slowly, ever so slowly, he undid the buttons on her nightgown, easing it open so he could touch her even more.

"You're getting warmer," he whispered.

"Yes."

"Beautiful. You're so beautiful," he said huskily, his deep voice reverberating against her. He started to lower his head to kiss her, but she put a trembling hand to his chest.

There was so much at stake. She was suddenly afraid of disappointing him. She thought about all the pictures she'd seen of him with half-dressed, sultry women hanging on him, their expressions and posture suggesting they'd just engaged in total intimacy.

He was waiting for her to say something. She was so afraid this wouldn't last, so afraid Sonny wouldn't let it. And she was afraid of saying or doing something that would ruin everything.

"Hi," she said.

He smiled, then laughed. "Hi."

His mouth was red from their shared kisses, his hair wet from the rain, and sexy as only Sonny's could be.

His eyes were dark with desire. "Now what were you *really* going to say?" he asked.

She was surprised that he'd read her so easily.

"Nothing."

"Emily—"

He bent his head and pressed his mouth to hers. She sensed reassurance in that kiss. He drew away enough to look into her eyes. "Second thoughts?" he asked, his hand across her rib cage, searing an outline on her flesh through the cotton of her gown.

"No. It's just that—" Heat rose in her cheeks. "It's just that I've never done this before," she confessed.

He smiled, and she thought there was something different about his smile. Then she realized the bitterness was gone. And there was such an unexpected tenderness in his expression that it made her throat hurt.

Then he said, "You know, sea treasure, I have the strangest feeling this will all be new to me, too."

Bless him.

He started to lower his head, then paused. Another smile. A teasing smile that completely beguiled her.

"Is the flame still burning?" he asked.

"Yes," she whispered. "It's still burning."

He was gentle with her. So gentle that Emily ended up pulling him closer, saying, "I want all of you—"

And then he touched her soul.

Chapter Twelve

Sonny had never been concerned with the hours lost to sleep. He usually welcomed them. But sleeping had suddenly become a waste of precious time. So he spent the hours until dawn awake, with a slumbering Emily in his arms.

Sometimes he would fall into a strange, half-awake state, but he never lost track of where he was. He was always aware of Emily, sweet and warm next to him. He could smell the scent of the ocean in her mermaid hair, hear her gentle dream sighs.

He was awake when the rain ceased its soft patter against the windows, awake when the night birds began singing, awake when the false light of early dawn began to creep into the room.

Emily was lying facing him, her hair draped over her shoulder like golden seaweed dried in the sun. Her coloring—it was as delicate as a sea shell's—all soft pinks and pale yellows. Her curling eyelashes were golden and lying against smooth cheeks.

Holding her in his arms, he felt as beguiled and mystified by her as he had that first day when he'd pulled her from the ocean. He'd stared into her unearthly eyes and felt the same fascinating fear: a fear that she might simply vanish.

She shifted in his arms. She would be waking soon. How would she react now that the night was over? Knowing Emily, he expected she would be shy. Maybe embarrassed.

He knew he should have spared her the awkwardness and left before now, but he hadn't been able to make himself. He wanted to leave her in sunshine, not darkness.

Another sigh escaped her parted lips. Then her eyes, with their golden tipped lashes, fluttered open. He found himself staring into deep pools of blue. Sleep-confused pools of blue.

Don't let her be sorry, he prayed. Please, don't let her be sorry.

"Hi," he said.

The worry lines between her eyebrows gentled. Her mouth curved into a soft smile. "Hi."

The lightness in his heart was almost unbearable in its intensity. He saw a pink blush darken her cheeks, and knew she was being brave, knew she was trying to overcome any self-consciousness she might be feeling.

Without tightening his hold, he kissed her. Carefully. Softly. Let it be all right, he prayed.

She placed a hand against the side of his face and looked at him, her magic eyes full of sincerity. "Sonny... it's okay."

"Are you sure, mermaid?"

"Yes."

"And what about you? Are *you* okay?"

"I'm—" She smiled, most likely at the total inadequacy of the word. "I'm *okay*. Better than okay."

"That's good." The relief—and some other emotion he wasn't ready to face yet—overwhelmed him.

Looking at her golden beauty, feeling her legs intertwined with his, the soft swell of her breasts against his chest, he wanted to make love to her again, in the pure morning light. But that would be going too fast. He didn't want to scare her. For Emily, he must take this slow. And because he knew her well enough to know she would still feel shy about getting dressed in front of him, he kissed her, then said, "I'm going to go put out the lighthouse lamps."

She blinked and nodded.

It took more willpower than he knew he possessed to draw away from her, to leave her lying there tousled and warm. But he did it. For Emily, he did it.

Emily lay in bed, watching Sonny slip into his clothes. Sunlight poured across him, turning his skin golden, outlining taut muscles. Memories of the night washed over her. He'd touched her with such tenderness.... She wanted him to lie back down beside her, hold her again, touch her again....

But this was new to her, and to ask him to stay would seem so bold. Too bold.

When he was dressed, he pressed a quick kiss on her mouth, but didn't touch her with his hands, didn't pull her close as she wished he would.

After he'd gone, she lay in bed, unwilling to let go of the night. Only yesterday she'd thought he was leaving St. Genevieve, leaving her. And now...

She tamped down her joy, tempered it with caution. Now, for all she knew, he could still be leaving.

Emotionally, she wanted to accept what had happened as a sign that Sonny was hers, and she was his. Later, when she knew things were *really* okay, she would shout. For now, her smiles would have to be quiet smiles.

She got up and took a shower. As she slipped into a gray skirt and a mauve sweater, she could hear the sound of banging pans and the smell of food coming from the kitchen.

That's where she found Sonny, in front of the stove, turning pancakes.

He was dressed in a clean pair of jeans and a black sweater. He looked up at her and smiled, and she felt her breath catch. It was his new smile. The one without the bitterness, without the self-mockery. This smile was as pure and innocent as the morning. This smile was for her.

She smiled back, feeling shaken and a little frightened by the intensity of her love for him.

And then he did something she would never have expected from Sonny. He put down the spatula and crossed to her in three long strides. Without hesitating, almost seeming as if he couldn't stop himself, he wrapped his arms around her and pulled her close, rocking her against his chest, murmuring her name in her hair.

Last night he'd been so wonderfully tender, wooing her with sweet words, gentle hands. Now her blood went warm and she realized she would like him to weave his magic again. Soon. Now.

But he pressed a kiss to her forehead, then let her go—almost reluctantly? She hoped it was reluctantly—then went back to his cooking.

"We don't have any syrup," he said. "How about jelly?"

"I'll make some syrup."

"You can make syrup?"

He seemed so amazed that somebody could make syrup that she laughed. "Yes. It's easy. I'll show you."

Side by side, they finished cooking breakfast, with Emily showing him how to make syrup from brown sugar.

They ate breakfast with the sunshine pouring in the lattice windows, making cheerful squares on the pinewood floor.

Normally Emily would have been anxious to get to her kite shop, but this morning she wanted to stay home, she wanted to stay with Sonny. What they had shared last night was too new. She was afraid it might not withstand the test of a single day of separation.

But the day followed the pattern they had unconsciously set from the beginning. As on all the other mornings, Sonny walked with her to the village. But this time, instead of walking her to the kite shop, he stopped when they came to the place where the cobblestone roads intersected.

"I'm going to use the drugstore phone to call the coast guard," he explained.

"Yes."

She needed to know if he planned to stay with her. If he planned to be her husband, her friend. "Are you going to work on the lighthouse today?" she asked instead.

"Yes, but I'll see you at noon," he promised. "Then I'll help you with the struts on the dragon kite. I've thought of a way to make them strong and flexible at the same time."

She smiled in relief. He wasn't leaving. Not today, anyway. Not tomorrow, she hoped, or the next day.

He was watching her. There was an expression in his eyes she'd seen many times, but hadn't recognized until now. He wanted to touch her. She glanced up and down the street. Too many people. She smiled, and he smiled. And she knew that he knew what she was thinking.

"Bye," he said.

"Bye."

He turned and headed down the cobblestone lane, toward the St. Genevieve drugstore.

She watched as he walked away, his hands in his pockets, sunlight glinting off the streaks in his hair. Her husband. Her love.

* * *

Sonny strolled along the wooden walkway. The sunshine was warm on his face, the breeze coming in off the ocean, crisp, refreshing.

Even though he'd been awake all night, he wasn't tired. Instead for the first time in years he felt alive.

As he made his way to the hub of the village, people passed, smiling and nodding. He would smile and nod in return, feeling as if they'd accepted him, that he was almost a part of their island. A part of Emily's island.

The good feeling ended as soon as he stepped inside the drugstore.

Something was wrong. He could feel it.

From behind the counter, Clayton said hello, but he acted funny. A little guilty. Sonny explained that he needed to make a call, and Clayton slid the old-fashioned black phone across the counter.

Sonny made the call, then pushed the phone back. "Thanks."

"No problem." But Clayton wouldn't look at him.

Something *was* wrong. Sonny hadn't imagined it.

Then, so quickly he almost didn't see it, Clayton's gaze flashed to something past Sonny, then away.

Sonny turned. Behind him was the magazine rack. Sonny's own face looked back at him from a cover. *Celebrity World.* The same magazine that had caused trouble before.

Above his face, in two inch letters was the headline: Sonny Maxwell Sold By Mother For Booze.

Sonny felt as if someone had kicked him in the stomach. It was hard for him to breathe.

He wasn't aware of reaching for the magazine, but suddenly there it was, in his hands. He was gripping it so tightly his knuckles were white.

He recognized the byline. Charlie Painter—the guy who had lied about Emily.

Sonny didn't read the article word for word. He didn't need to. It was all there. His ugly past. Somehow the reporter had found Evie, the woman who used to run the home. Just reading her name made him feel queasy, the way he used to feel whenever Evie yelled at him. Not that she'd ever hit him. She hadn't. But not a day had gone by that she didn't let him know just how worthless he was.

Up until now Sonny had thought that nobody could get to him anymore. He thought he was immune to pain-laden words. But that had been before Emily had come into his life and made him feel again.

He hadn't wanted her to know about his mother, or about Evie. And now it was all here. In black and white.

Emily.

Now she would know just how unworthy he was. Now she would know the real Sonny Maxwell. He hated himself for dragging her down with him. Her life had been so pure, so clean before she met him. And then he'd come and touched her with his ugliness.

"You okay, Sonny?" came Clayton's voice, penetrating his bleak thoughts.

No. I'll never be okay.

Sonny grabbed the rest of the magazines from the rack, tossed a ten-dollar bill on the counter—enough to cover the magazines and the phone call—and left.

He walked blindly. Hours may have passed, but he was unaware of time. Finally, he found himself on a street that led north, to the lighthouse, or south. . . .

He looked down at the magazines he was still clutching in his hand. He didn't know why he'd bought them, didn't know why he'd ever thought he could keep something like that from Emily.

He thought about the way she'd looked at him this morning. It had filled his heart with joy, pure and sweet and aching.

She would never look at him that way again.

He couldn't go back. He couldn't face her.

He tossed the papers in a cast-iron trash container, then looked south, down the narrow lane. It led to the pier, to the harbor, to the boats that could carry him away.

Emily's kite was already up. The purple unicorn again. It seemed to be one of her favorites. She was rather like a unicorn herself. Gentle. Noble. Innocent. Easily hurt.

He had been the selfish human who had captured her in order to steal her magic.

Emily.

He started walking toward the harbor, toward the boats that would carry him away.

* * *

Emily sat in the kite shop, staring blankly at the silent sewing machine. She'd given up all pretense of work. It was impossible to concentrate.

Where was Sonny?

He said he'd be there at noon, and it was one-thirty. Maybe the coastguard had come and he'd been detained, she reasoned. Yes. That must be what had happened. He would come later.

But the afternoon sunlight crept across the planked floor, catching the tiny crystal kite that hung in the window, its prisms breaking the light into miniature rainbows that flickered around the room. Babbie called them fairies. . . .

The sun moved on, taking Babbie's fairies with it. And still Sonny didn't come.

Even though she tried to put it from her mind, one thought kept coming back. What if he'd left the island? What if he'd left *her?*

No. He couldn't. Not now. Not after last night.

By four o'clock Sonny still hadn't come and Emily decided to close early. She put things away, then went into the makeshift kitchen and switched off the light. The bell on the front door jingled and she hurried to the front room, expecting Sonny.

But it was her father who stepped inside, closing the door behind him, bringing along cool air and smells of the salt sea.

The feeling of dread intensified. She hurried to her father. "What's wrong? Is it one of the girls?"

He removed his seaman's cap and gripped it tightly in both hands. "No. The girls are fine."

"Sonny? It's Sonny, isn't it?"

He looked at her, his weather-lined face sad. "Sonny's gone back to the mainland, Emily."

Denial screamed in her. No. He said he'd be back. He'd looked at her in a special way, a way that had been meant for her alone. "Are you sure?" she managed to ask, her throat tight.

"Aye. I'm sorry, lass. I saw him just before he left. He said to tell you goodbye."

"Goodbye? But he's coming back, isn't he? Did he say when he'd be back?"

Her father looked around the small room, as if he couldn't stand to face the sadness in his daughter's eyes.

"Papa—tell me."

"Ah, Emily." His shoulders slouched in defeat. "He said he didn't know if he was coming back."

"I see," she said slowly, eyes wide, focusing on nothing. She had to pull herself together, get through these next few minutes, the next few hours, the next few days. "Well . . . I was just closing up . . . I have to bring in the kite."

"I'm sorry, lass."

"I just need to find the key. Where did I put the key? I had it just a moment ago."

Her father handed it to her. "Why not come home with me? The girls would like to see you."

"I'm okay, Papa. Really."

He walked with her to the wharf, to help her take down the kite. When it was safely tucked under Emily's arm, he reached deep into the pocket of his wool jacket and pulled out a folded magazine. "No sense in you hearing about this from somebody else," he said, handing it to her. Then he headed up the lane that led to his gray, two-story house.

On the way back to the point, Emily opened the folded magazine to find Sonny's face staring up at her.

She tried to swallow the pain in her throat, but it only made it hurt more.

The photo was classic Sonny Maxwell. Sexy. A little tousled, a little unkempt—enough to make women wonder what he'd just been doing. And like most of his pictures, it seemed as if the camera had accidently caught something nobody was supposed to see: a haunting bleakness.

She forced her gaze from his face to the article. It wasn't anything she didn't already know. But to read it in cold, clipped, journalistic prose made it seem all the more heartbreaking.

It told of his childhood and how his mother had given him away. It told of his poor acting ability, and the way he'd shown no emotion when he'd been told of his mother's death. *Poor Sonny*.

Poor me.

By the time she reached the cottage, the sky and ocean were washed in a gray light. The Jeep was still parked near the gate, where it had been this morning. Seeing it there gave her a small burst of hope. Maybe he would be back.

Out off the point, the electronic buoy was back in working order. It almost seemed as if last night had never happened.

As soon as she stepped inside the cottage, she felt the emptiness. It was all around her. It was inside her.

Not wanting to go any farther right now, she sat down on the church pew near the door.

Had he left because of the article? No, he had planned to leave anyway. He'd said so last night. This morning she had felt as if they were finally husband and wife. But their night together had meant nothing to Sonny, at least nothing more than other nights spent with other women.

Her tear-blurred gaze fell upon the lighthouse logbook. She picked it up and hugged it to her. Then she began leafing through the stiff pages, hoping to derive some small measure of comfort from the words inside. She turned the pages, not really seeing anything until something unusual caught her eye. She went back to the last ink-marked page and recognized Sonny's strong, square handwriting. Yesterday's date was in the left-hand column. Beside it, just below her grandfather's name, Sonny had added a new entry, the name of the most recent keeper of the light: Emily Christian Maxwell.

Chapter Thirteen

The next day Emily used her father's phone to call Doreen. When no one answered, she tried Martin's office. He was out, so she left a message with his secretary.

Two hours later Martin called back and Emily explained what had happened.

"I'm going to stick my neck out and get personal here," Martin said. "As you're well aware of, Sonny doesn't talk about himself. In all the years I've known him, he's never said a word about his past. I don't think he wants anybody to know about it, especially you, somebody he really cares about."

Emily made a protesting sound, but Martin continued.

"Sonny comes from a dysfunctional family. He had no father. His mother was an alcoholic. People from dysfunctional families wear this facade that they don't want anyone to see behind. Not because they are private people, but because they are afraid no one will like the person they are inside. They can give love, they just have a hard time accepting it because they think they are unworthy.''

''How can you be so sure Sonny is like that?'' Then she voiced her greatest fear. ''Maybe he just grew tired of me.''

''I know because I'm like him. I came from a similar background. Here I am, supposed to be one of the best doctors in the area, but in my own mind, I'm still that little kid who wet the bed.''

She would never have guessed.

''I have an idea that Sonny saw the article and ran,'' Martin said. ''We're always looking for an excuse to say—'see, you can't love me. I'm unlovable.' In fact, I lost my wife because I couldn't accept her love.''

Martin Berlin, of all people—unsure of himself? He seemed so totally confident. ''What should I do?'' Emily asked.

''I'd say, give him a little time. If he doesn't come back, you might have to go to him.''

Which meant waiting. And she knew that this waiting would be some of the hardest she'd ever done.

Somebody was pounding on the door.

Go away.

Sonny shifted his position on the couch, heels of his bare feet propped on the arm. It wasn't comfortable. But he wasn't looking for comfort.

He'd briefly thought about going to the cabin, but had quickly dumped that idea. It would remind him of Emily. So he'd chosen his apartment. Emily had never been to his apartment.

The pounding continued.

"I don't want any!" he shouted.

But it wouldn't stop.

"Okay, okay." He levered himself up, trudged to the door and jerked it open.

Doreen. He should have known.

"What do you want?" he asked.

"You look like hell," she said, shoving past him.

"What do you want?" He slammed the door and followed her to the sitting room.

"You know what's annoying?" she asked as she shoved a stack of newspapers off a chair. "Even when you look like hell, you look good. Makes me sick." She sat down. "So, Martin says you and Emily had a little tiff."

"A tiff? We didn't have any *tiff*." He raked his fingers through his hair, then rubbed his stubbled chin. When was the last time he'd taken a shower?

He plopped down on the couch. Stacked precariously on top of the cluttered table were three cans of cola attached to a plastic holder. He tugged one free of the plastic ring. "Is that Ireland job still open?" he asked. He offered a can to Doreen, but she shook her head.

"Sonny, you're a fool, sabotaging your life like this. Emily is the best thing that ever happened to you."

"I know." He took a swig of warm cola, made a face and swallowed. "The problem is, I'm the worst thing that ever happened to her." He laughed, his old bitter laugh. "Funny how that works, isn't it?"

Doreen made a disgusted face. "I could just shake you till your teeth rattle!"

"I'm doing Emily a favor by getting out of her life. Didn't you hear?" He pointed to the copy of *Celebrity World* lying on the table. "I'm a loser."

"Doesn't Emily get any say in this? After all, she loves you."

He waved the words away with one hand. "She doesn't love me. Let's change the subject. What about that Ireland job?"

"If you're running—"

"I'm not running."

"—because of what that rag said, you're crazy. If you think Emily learned something she didn't already know, you're wrong."

He looked directly at her, ready to come clean for once. "I didn't want her to know." It was the closest he'd ever come to a confession in his life.

"Is it impossible for you to believe she might love you in spite of all your shortcomings?"

"Yes."

"Sonny, I told her about you a long time ago. Not all of it, but most of what I've been able to piece together over the years. She knew about your mother and that hellhole you grew up in."

Not Doreen. He couldn't believe Doreen would betray him like that. He'd never said it in words, but over the past several years he'd come to think of her as a friend. And now... now to find she'd stabbed him in the back like this....

"Get the hell out of here," he told her quietly.

"I'll leave. But before I do, I have something to show you." She dug through the big leather bag of hers and pulled out some curled black and white proofs. She stood up, tossing them down on the table. "I took those pictures thinking to show them to one of the magazines and possibly get Emily to do some modeling. But when I developed them I realized they were too personal, too revealing. To have allowed anyone outside Emily's family to see them would have been an invasion of privacy."

She moved to the door. "Emily has the most wonderfully transparent face I've ever seen. It's as if every thought can be seen in her expression."

Sonny picked up the pictures. Three in all. All of Emily. They had been taken at the same time. In every shot she was watching something off camera, staring into the distance, her hair in sea-damp tendrils about her face. And in her beautiful, magic eyes was a longing so deep, and so haunting that he could feel her pain. Feel her love.

"When were these taken?" Sonny asked, amazed that his voice sounded anywhere near normal. He felt sick inside. His stomach muscles tightened as he fought to stabilize his emotions, fought to push aside the grief and deep sense of loss, fought to ignore the jealousy he felt toward the unknown person who had all of Emily's attention. Who had Emily's love.

"I took them a few weeks ago."

He had to ask, had to know. "Who . . . who is she looking at?"

Doreen turned the doorknob, poised to leave. "You, Sonny. She's looking at you."

Chapter Fourteen

The weather had turned warm. A breeze blew in from across the ocean, tugging at Emily's sundress, whipping it around her bare knees as she worked in the garden. Even though her hair was tied back, she could feel damp curls escaping around her face. Absentmindedly, she pushed them away, only to have the wind push them back.

She was picking leaf lettuce and spinach, laying the leaves in an oblong basket—making a contrast of light and dark green.

As she worked, the smell of damp earth drifted up to her, taking her back to another day, to the day she'd found Sonny planting onions upside down. She'd had a heart full of hope that day. She'd been a child that day.

I can wait, Sonny had told her. She had believed him because she'd wanted to believe him, because she'd needed to believe him.

Martin said Sonny cared for her, but Emily was plagued with doubt. Martin wasn't aware of what had passed the night before Sonny returned to the mainland. He didn't know that Sonny may have left for a totally different reason than fear of love.

She was new to love between a man and a woman. And Sonny had known so many gorgeous models. She was afraid that she had seemed an inexperienced child to him.

He'd been gone but five days. It seemed like five months. Martin had told her she might need to go to Sonny, but she wasn't that kind of person. She didn't have that kind of confidence. If she could be sure Sonny cared for her, then she would feel differently. But she wasn't sure. She wasn't sure at all.

And deep down, she wanted it to be his choice. She wanted him to choose to come back to her.

She straightened, her gaze drawn to the yellow sloping hills that flanked the lane leading to the village. Normally early summer when the hillsides were covered with huge, teacup-size dandelions was her favorite time of year. But today the sight of the vivid yellow hills failed to warm her heart.

Far off in the distance, her eye caught a silhouette against the cloudless blue sky. Someone had crested the hilltop and was walking through the yellow field, coming her direction.

Poor Papa.

He came to check on her every day. She hated to have him worry, but there was nothing she could do. It was only natural to worry about the ones you love.

But as the figure drew nearer, she saw that the stride was not her father's. And the shoulders were not her father's.

And then she saw sunlight glinting off sun-lightened hair.

Sonny.

The basket slipped from her fingers. She took a few steps, then stopped, unsure. Why had he come? Was he here to stay? Or was he here to tell her goodbye?

Her heart hammered madly against her rib cage. Sweat broke out on her skin to be instantly dried by the wind.

Wait, she told herself. Wait and see what's in his heart.

She'd almost forgotten how beautiful he was, how effortless his movements. As he neared, she could see the wind making ripples across his white shirt. It lifted his hair, tossing it across his forehead.

She loved him so much.

Please don't let this be goodbye. Please don't break my heart.

And then he stopped a few yards from her, close enough for her to feel the grayness of his sorrow, to see that his eyes were clear and intense, that the remoteness that often filled them was gone.

But—*oh, Sonny*— He looked so sad, so haunted that she wanted to cry for him.

She could sense a deep longing swirling about them. But was it his longing she felt, or only her own?

"I forgot something," he said quietly.

She could only stand there, frozen, stunned. Too hurt to speak, too numb to move. So, he hadn't come back to her. He had simply forgotten something.

What would she do? How would she face the rest of her life without him? In her mind, she visualized where she'd written his name beside hers in the log book. In ink. She shouldn't have written it in ink.

She turned away, hurried back to the garden. On her knees, she gathered up the basket, picking up the leaves that had scattered.

Bruised leaves.

"Emily—"

His hoarse voice, sounding deeper than deep, came from nearby, penetrating her black despair, but did nothing to alleviate the pain. Then his hand was there, stopping her frantic struggles.

Gentle fingers touched her jaw, tilting her head up. Tears swam in her eyes. She blinked and swallowed, staring into his gray-blue sorrow.

"Don't you want to know what I forgot?"

She shook her head, unable to speak.

"I'll tell you anyway." He pulled her to her feet so that she stood facing him, her skirt billowing out, tangling with his legs. And then he said, "I forgot to tell you . . . that I love you."

Her mind stopped its anguished rampage. She feared she had simply wished the words, imagined them in the chaos of her mind. "What?"

"I didn't leave because of you," he said. "I left because of me. I was ashamed. I was afraid. I didn't think somebody like you could ever love somebody like me."

"Oh, Sonny. How could I *not* love you? I wish you could understand just how special you are. There is nothing you could have ever said or done in your past that would change who you are right now, nothing that would ever make me stop loving you."

"It's hard for me to believe . . . to trust . . ."

"Trust me, Sonny. You can always trust me."

"I want to. I need to."

But he didn't move to hold her, seeming unsure.

Emily had to say what was in her heart. "You can leave if you grow tired of me," she said. "Leave if you need something more in your life. But don't ever leave for fear that I've stopped loving you. No matter how far you go, or how many times you run, I'll always be here, waiting. I'll always love you."

The eyes that looked down at her were filled with so much love that they took her breath away.

"You and our life together are all I want," he said. "It's more than I ever dreamed, more than I deserve. I could no more grow tired of you than I could grow tired of sunshine. I *need* you. You are the best, the most real thing that's ever happened to me. I'll love you forever, Emily. I'll need you forever. Next time I won't run away, I'll run *to* you," he said, his deep voice cracking with emotion.

Wondrous, wondrous magic.

He wrapped his arms around her and pressed her to his chest, holding her tightly, as if he couldn't get close enough. Slowly he lowered his head. Then his lips, soft and warm, moved over hers, making it all true.

Epilogue

Emily and Sonny stood in the middle of the dandelion field. Emily looked over at her husband. He was wearing a blue-gray sweater that perfectly matched his eyes. Last week he'd worn it to the photography showing Doreen had arranged. He'd told everyone that Emily had made it for him, seeming more proud of the sweater than of his beautiful photographs.

Now his head was bent as his long, pianist's fingers worked with the kite string. He looked up. "Ready?"

"Ready."

Together they had built a dragon kite that was four times as big as Emily's original. Sonny had devised a way to fly it using two sets of string. Now he handed one spool to Emily while he took the other.

"We have to let the string out at the same speed."

She nodded.

They stood side by side. Emily gripped her spool with both hands, feeling a heavy tug as the wind breathed life into the huge dragon. The kite lifted, the string singing as it fed out.

Excitement vibrated around them.

"It's working!" Sonny shouted.

She laughed in unrestrained joy. "I told you it would!"

He looked over at her and smiled, a smile as pure as sunlight. Then the wind circled, whirling the kaleidoscope of his colors around her.

*   *   *   *   *

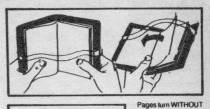

FOUR UNIQUE SERIES
FOR EVERY WOMAN YOU ARE . . .

Silhouette Romance®

Love, at its most tender, provocative,
emotional . . . in stories that will make you laugh and
cry while bringing you the magic of falling in love.

*6 titles
per month*

Silhouette Special Edition®

Sophisticated, substantial and packed with
emotion, these powerful novels of life and love will
capture your imagination and steal your heart.

*6 titles
per month*

SILHOUETTE *Desire*®

Open the door to romance and passion. Humorous,
emotional, compelling—yet always a believable
and sensuous story—Silhouette Desire never
fails to deliver on the promise of love.

*6 titles
per month*

SILHOUETTE·INTIMATE·MOMENTS®

Enter a world of excitement, of romance
heightened by suspense, adventure and the
passions every woman dreams of. Let us
sweep you away.

*4 titles
per month*